NANCY WARREN

FAIR ISLE
AND FORTUNES

VAMPIRE KNITTING CLUB
BOOK SIX

FAIR ISLE AND FORTUNES, Vampire Knitting Club Book 6, Copyright ©
2019 by Nancy Warren

ISBN: ebook 978-1-928145-58-5

ISBN: print 978-1-928145-57-8

ISBN: hardcover 978-1-990210-30-3

Cover Design by Lou Harper of Cover Affairs

Ambleside Publishing

INTRODUCTION

What if the fortune teller at the local village fair is a witch? And all her fortunes come true—even when she foresees a death...

When Lucy Swift's cousin Violet decides to take over as the fortune teller at Moreton-under-Wychwood's annual summer fête, Lucy thinks being her assistant will be a fun way to spend a Saturday. That is, until someone's murdered, and the locals turn on Violet who foresaw the death.

To save her, Lucy and her band of undead amateur sleuths have to find out what's really going on in this charming Cotswolds village. What better way than to offer knitting classes? No one has to know that the teacher is a vampire.

But uncovering the dark secrets under the postcard-prettiness will bring great danger to Lucy and those she loves.

Fair Isle and Fortunes can be read as a stand-alone mystery in this best-selling series. There's no violence or gore, just a good, clean mystery, with a lot of fun, a crazy-smart cat, tangled knitting, and a few laughs.

$\sim$

The best way to keep up with new releases and special offers is to join Nancy's newsletter at NancyWarrenAuthor.com.

FAIR ISLE AND FORTUNES

CHAPTER 1

*T*he village fête at Moreton-Under-Wychwood was the highlight of the social calendar in that small Cotswold village—at least for most villagers. For the coven, of course, the solstice events that took place at the nearby standing stones took precedence.

The community fair drew locals, families and fairgoers from miles around. I'd never been to a village fête before, so I was excited when my cousin Violet suggested I accompany her.

"I'm going to be telling fortunes, and I'll need someone to show people in and take the money." She grinned, flipping her black hair over her shoulder so the stripe of bright pink and purple fluttered like a banner. "You can be *my* assistant for a change."

"Do you make much money telling fortunes?"

"I don't know. I've never done it before. The fortunes used to be told by Madame Tatania, who was really Elsie Thompkins and whose husband runs a local pub. But Elsie's in Dublin with her daughter, who's having a baby, so they need a new fortune-teller."

"What fun. Do you have any experience?"

Violet raised her brows and put her hands on her hips. "Lucy, I'm a witch. I think that qualifies me quite nicely. You can watch and learn." Vi had an annoying way of always reminding me she'd been a practicing witch longer than I had, though after February's disaster of the love potions, I didn't know how she had the nerve to pull the superior witch act with me.

Still, I was enjoying getting to know the countryside around my Oxford shop, and it would be fun to spend a Saturday at a village fair. I still had to run Cardinal Woolsey's yarn and knitting shop, though, so I asked Violet what she thought I might do for an assistant. Truth was, I'd had some bad luck with assistants. If they didn't turn out to be murderers or soul-sucking demons, they had a tendency to leave. I didn't think I was a bad employer, more that I couldn't seem to choose the kind of people who stayed.

I'd had the same problem with the men in my life. At least, the mortal ones. Rafe Crosyer, the five-hundred-year-old vampire, would stick around forever. Literally. The trouble with our relationship was that I wouldn't. It sounded romantic to think of letting him turn me so we could live together forever, but the reality, as I knew from daily experience, was that living forever wasn't as thrilling as you might think. Mortals that vampires cared about died. They couldn't live for too long in one place, or people became suspicious that they weren't aging, so they had to move every generation or so.

However, the biggest issue I saw was boredom. The vampires living in the tunnels under my Oxford shop all had more money than they could ever spend—Einstein was right about the power of time and compound interest. They'd seen and done pretty much everything, and they no longer needed to hunt thanks to blood banks and modern technology.

They were rich, strong and bored. Also, in Rafe's case, bossy and controlling. I knew he meant well and had my safety in mind, but I was an independent woman of the modern age.

When he was growing up, women were the property of their menfolk. He tried to keep up with the times, but we butted heads more often than I'd have liked.

However, even knowing all that, I was incredibly drawn to Rafe. He was gorgeous, sexy and smart. Him being a controlling know-it-all wouldn't have been so bad if he hadn't, in fact, known just about everything. At least I had him beat on modern culture, and some of the most fun we had was seeing movies that he'd been too snobbish to bother with.

Since Violet was supposed to be my assistant, I thought it was only fair she should come up with her Saturday replacement. Especially if she was going to drag me away from the shop, too. She wrinkled her nose. "What about Alice? Don't you think she owes us a favor after we made Charlie fall in love with her?"

I could not believe that Violet was suggesting Alice owed us anything after her beloved had nearly ended up in jail for murder. Still, Alice was such a nice person, she might actually do it, if she wasn't already committed to working in the bookstore across the street on Saturday.

"I really need to hire another proper assistant." We both glanced toward the front window where I had taped a Help Wanted notice. I'd had the paper laminated, as I seemed to put it in the window so often.

I'd put another notice up at the local grocers, but so far there hadn't been any takers. The trouble was, a warm and cozy wool shop in Oxford was a wonderful place to work in the cold weather, but, as I was learning, it wasn't so exciting when the weather turned warm. When I walked around Oxford and saw the flowers blooming, sending their scent into the air, and felt the sun on my face, I didn't relish being cooped up with woolen goods all day. I suspected that most people who might like a part-time job at Cardinal Woolsey's felt the same way.

However, I needed to find a reliable assistant and soon.

At that moment I heard noises in the back room of my shop, which suggested we had visitors. Sure enough, after surreptitiously peeping from behind the curtain, two of my favorite vampires, Sylvia and my grandmother, walked into the shop.

Sylvia beamed at us. "We were just getting ready for bed, and we thought we might do some knitting first. I'm completely out of the purple cashmere yarn."

Gran came behind her. "And I was thinking I might crochet you a nice lace tablecloth, Lucy. It would be lovely on the dining table upstairs."

I couldn't believe my ears. "You want to crochet a tablecloth? Won't that take forever?" The minute I said the words, I could've bitten my tongue. She sighed and said, "I hope so."

Ouch. To cover my blunder I rushed forward and said, "This ecru cotton is new. I think it would give a look of antique lace."

She brightened immediately. Gran always loved to stay on top of new products in the store she used to own. "It's lovely, dear." She picked up one of the balls and turned it over in her hands. "Who's the supplier?" Then of course we had to talk about sales and the latest stock. It was nice to be able to discuss business with the woman who used to own the shop.

I sighed. "My biggest problem right now is that I need an assistant. Violet wants me to go to the village fête at Moreton-Under-Wychwood on Saturday, but I don't think I can go. I've got no one to watch Cardinal Woolsey's."

She and Sylvia looked at each other. "We'll do it."

I telegraphed distress to Sylvia. Gran could not be seen in public. She tended to forget that a lot of the people who shopped here used to be her customers. Finding Gran alive after they had cried at her funeral would not be conducive to good business.

Sylvia understood my dilemma immediately and said, "But, Agnes, have you forgotten? You're going to Dublin this weekend. You and Mabel."

Gran's forehead creased in puzzlement. "Dublin? Did I know about this?"

Since Gran could be a bit forgetful, Sylvia took shameless advantage. "Of course you did. You're meeting up with Mary and Sheila, those lovely women we met last time we were there."

She explained to me and Violet, "Mary owns a lovely old manor house in the country about an hour outside of Dublin. Agnes and Mabel are going to spend the whole weekend doing crafts." As my grandmother was still looking confused, she said, "Agnes, why don't you take along some of this lovely cotton and demonstrate to everyone how to make lace? I'll bet some of them don't know how."

Gran brightened immediately. "What a good idea. I do miss teaching my classes."

When they'd gathered their supplies, Sylvia came close to me and whispered, "Now I've got to scramble about and put together a crafts weekend in Dublin. And talk Mabel into going."

I thanked her in an equally soft voice. Then she said, "Why don't you ask Clara to run the shop for you? She's very good. So long as she naps the night before, she should be all right for the day."

I agreed that this was a good idea, but I still felt I needed a proper assistant. One who wasn't going to yawn all through the day.

Even Nyx, my black cat familiar, wasn't lazing about in the front window as often as she had during the cold weather. She came and went from an open window during the night, and often when I got up the next morning she still hadn't returned home. She came back when she felt like it, and if she was bored or lonely, I would hear her meowing through the door that connected the shop and my upstairs flat.

I'd let her in and she'd yawn, do a circle of the shop making sure no mice had sneaked in when she wasn't on patrol, and then, job done, she'd jump into the front window and curl up in the sun.

Since I needed to get out and get some sun myself, I walked across the street and up the block to Frogg's Books, hoping to talk Alice into watching the shop for the day. She was an excellent knitter and had taught a few beginner classes. I'd barely had a moment to feel the warm sun on my face and my bare arms when I saw Scarlett Baker and her friend Polly walking toward me. They were both students at Cardinal College, which was on the same street as my shop. We'd become friendly during a recent college production of *A Midsummer Night's Dream*. The production had been fraught with disaster but, surprisingly, that had brought us closer.

They both waved to me, and Scarlett said, "Lucy! Don't tell me you're leaving? We were coming to see you."

I stood in the middle of the sidewalk and waited for them to reach me. Polly said, "We were coming into your shop. Scarlett's teaching me how to knit. I'm trying to quit smoking, you see, and I must have something to do with my hands."

Scarlett looked at her with affection. "The not smoking's also making her grumpy, and I'm hoping knitting will be a soothing activity."

I was very pleased Polly was quitting smoking, of course, but even more pleased to discover that Scarlett could knit. "How come you never told me you could knit?"

She shook her head. "We were so busy with the play, I never really thought about it. I've been knitting since I was a child. It was only when Polly was desperately looking for something else to do with her hands—"

"Other than using them to open packets of sweets and crisps," Polly interjected. "I was getting so fat."

"I thought of knitting. Polly loves it, and it's something we can do together during boring lectures or while watching the telly."

Naturally, I was always delighted to bring more customers into my shop, but I was even more thrilled at the possibility that a local university student might be interested in a part-time job. I asked Scarlett on the spot if I could hire her, explaining that I needed a second assistant mainly for Saturdays and the odd extra shift at a mutually convenient time.

They looked at each other and burst out laughing. "I've been wanting to get a part-time job. Polly told me I should ask you, but I was too shy."

Now it was my turn to laugh. "Perfect. You're hired."

"That's it? That's the entire job interview?"

Now that she mentioned it, I was a very lax employer. No wonder I kept losing my assistants. Scarlett was an actress who liked drama, but I also knew that she was cheerful, gorgeous, and good with people.

When you've been through a frightening experience with someone, you get to know them, and Scarlett was a good person. "Let's try it and see how it goes. Perhaps you can start a week from Saturday? If you come in a bit early, I'll explain how the till works and so on."

"That's fantastic," they both said at once.

I couldn't believe how easy this had been. I felt so magnanimous, I told them that as a signing bonus, I'd give them both the employee discount on whatever they bought.

It didn't solve the problem of this Saturday, but I was fairly certain Mabel and Clara would cover for me for the one day I was at the fair.

It was only one day, after all. So long as they were well fed, how much damage could a pair of vampires do in one day?

CHAPTER 2

*W*hen I inherited Cardinal Woolsey's and the flat above it, I also reluctantly ended up with Gran's tiny Ford. I'd grown up in the States, and learned to drive there, but I was getting better at driving on the *wrong* side of the road so long as I didn't let my thoughts wander. On that Saturday morning in early June, I drove carefully from Oxford to Moreton-Under-Wychwood, a small town about ten miles away. I pulled the tiny old car into the Pig and Plough pub's parking lot, which had been given over for the day to patrons of the village fête. Fortunately, the weather had blessed the event. It was sunny with only a few clouds in the sky, just enough to give it atmosphere.

The village green was normally nothing more than a huge round grass field with a stream running through it. A few ancient trees, a mostly blank community noticeboard and a couple of benches were the main features. However, the small town had grown around the village green. The church, first built in the middle ages, was directly across the street, with its equally ancient graveyard. Cottages and houses built in honey-colored Cotswold stone ringed the green. They were from different eras, though the most modern was probably Victorian. There was a pub, where I'd just parked, a coffee shop, a post office and a co-op grocery store. Today, the village green was crowded with tents and people, games and food trucks and children running about laughing.

I liked to dress in hand-knitted sweaters whenever possible as a way of always advertising Cardinal Woolsey's. I thought of myself as a walking sandwich board when I was out, but it was a warm day, and I couldn't stand the thought of a thick jumper, so I'd thrown a white cashmere pashmina over a black T-shirt. Since I was going to be an assistant to a fortune-teller, I thought the shawl added more glamor than a cardigan.

I passed a stall draped with bunting of the British flag selling delicious-smelling pies, another where children were having their faces painted, and a booth where you had to throw balls and try to knock pins down in order to win a prize. Across the way, I could see a Punch and Judy show setting up.

I walked over the ancient wooden bridge that crossed a small stream. An old pump was beside it, and a tourist information sign that explained this was where the whole village used to come for water. I always loved these little glimpses into history.

The tents were all similar, white with red stripes down them, which added to the atmosphere of joyousness in the air. I decided to take a complete turn and look at all the booths before beginning my shift with Violet who, I was fairly certain, would be a tough taskmaster.

A band was warming up. At least, I hoped the discordant sounds meant they were warming up. They were down at one end of the village green beside where an archery club was setting up. I'd done some archery back at summer camp and thought, if I got a break, I might try my hand.

I was walking past a white elephant booth, which I'd have called a flea market. There were all kinds of junk in there:

small bits of furniture, vases, pictures, an old gramophone, books, old records, a glass case of costume jewelry, watches, old pipes and things. My attention was caught, or more like riveted, by a lamp. It wasn't an ordinary lamp. The base was a ceramic poodle in pink, with a badly painted face, wearing a tattered green bow around its neck. The lamp shade was pink to match and had plastic pink roses around the edge of the shade. It was, without doubt, the ugliest thing I had ever seen.

A woman of about fifty with soft red hair and wearing a blue polka-dot blouse over white slacks walked up. "It's quite a conversation piece, isn't it?"

"I can't find the words."

"We're not officially open yet, but I can put this aside for you, if you'd like it."

I backed away. "No. That's all right. I don't want to rob someone else of such a great piece."

I turned and picked my way past a collection of old stools and fireplace accessories when a man's voice hailed me.

I glanced up and smiled when I saw Liam. Another student from Cardinal College, he'd played Puck in *A Midsummer Night's Dream*. We'd come to recognize each other's specialness in the same way members of a secret society recognize a ring.

"Liam, good to see you. Do you live around here?"

"My people are from Ireland, but I've cousins living here." His eyes squinted at me with mischief. "As, I believe, do you."

Of course my cousin Violet and my great aunt Lavinia lived here, and my sometime mentor and oftentimes trickster rival Margaret Twig lived not too far away.

He said, "I didn't see you at the last coven potluck."

I shuddered. "After the disaster of the love potion, I didn't dare show my face. Besides, until I master my magic better, I'll always feel like the odd witch out."

He began to chuckle. "You're quite famous, you know. I wish

I'd been there when you sent the head standing stone flying through the air."

I shuddered again. "Don't remind me. It was mortifying."

His eyes lost their gleam of wickedness and went serious. "Also incredibly powerful. For all our sakes, you need to focus on your studies. You never know when we'll need someone of your power to defend and protect us."

"But you have Margaret Twig," I said. I might not like the woman, but no one could deny her power.

He said something I'd heard on several occasions. "You are a more powerful witch than Margaret Twig will ever be. That's why you threaten her."

Most earnestly I assured him that I did not want a showdown with Margaret Twig. She was welcome to remain the head of our coven. More than welcome. I didn't want to be head witch any more than I wanted to be a witch at all. It wasn't like I'd had a choice.

He carried a garment bag, and I asked, "Are you performing here?"

"Never miss an opportunity to make a fool of myself. I'll be putting on a magic show."

I raised my eyebrows at that. I might not be head witch, but I knew that we frowned on sharing our secrets with people in the normal world. At my expression, he laughed. "Don't worry, all the tricks I'll be doing you can get out of a book or, these days, on the Internet."

"Really?"

"You'd be amazed what you can find on YouTube. Though I know for a fact that anybody who reveals too much finds their channel mysteriously 'taken down.'" He put the 'taken down' in air quotes. I wondered if part of his role in life was to keep an eye on those who gave too much away. Vaguely, I assumed there must be some kind of an informal police force, some bureau of magical standards.

I told him I'd try to catch his act, and when he asked me where I was going, I explained about the fortune-telling booth.

He looked puzzled. "I thought Madame Tatania was back in my hometown. She's going to be a grandmother again. I heard she wasn't doing fortune-telling this year."

"She's not. My cousin Violet is standing in for her."

He sent me an odd look. "Your cousin Violet? Here?"

"Yes. Tent number thirty-two. I'm on my way there now. Do you know Violet?"

"We've met." The way he said the words with such airy dismissiveness told me immediately there was a story there. However, since he was a man and not related to me, I doubted he would tell me. I'd have to ask Vi.

When I asked him if he wanted to come with me and say hello to Violet, he promptly declined my offer, thus confirming my suspicion that there was a story there.

And don't I love a good gossip as much as the next witch?

I FOUND Violet's tent with no trouble. She'd decorated it with scarves and bells and a few dangling crystals, and Theodore, one of the vampire knitters with a talent for scene painting, had made her a silk banner. It was a thing of beauty, of dark purple silk decorated with gold paint and plastic jewels that caught the sunlight and sparkled.

I stepped inside the tent and discovered my cousin had truly embraced her day's calling. Her eyes were heavily made up, so they looked huge and smoky. She wore a red and gold silk turban and thick gold hoops in her ears. Her dress was actually a silk dressing gown that she'd borrowed from Alfred, one of the vampires who was given to colorful lounge wear.

She was in the act of throwing a lace cloth over a round patio table.

She greeted me, then asked, "What do you think of my crystal ball?"

I would never have guessed that was supposed to be a crystal ball. "It looks like a goldfish bowl turned upside down over a tea light."

Violet rolled her eyes. "Lucy, use your imagination."

"Maybe if you put a scarf over it?" I thought even an interesting glass paperweight would have been better.

Violet dug through a cloth grocery bag and found a creased white silk scarf. "I thought Madame Tatania would lend me her crystal ball, but apparently, she's very possessive. Says it's been in her family for generations and I might dilute its power. Honestly, what is it with mortals? They read a few horoscopes and do a couple of Tarot card readings, and suddenly they're convinced they have power. I could have shown her what real power looks like." At my gasp of distress, her blood-red lips curved in a smile. "Don't worry. I only messed up her suitcase a little."

When we'd fashioned the scarf around the fishbowl, it didn't look too bad. Then Violet looked at me and shook her head. "You should be in costume, too."

"I thought the pashmina added a touch of glamor."

"Not enough glam for Madame Violetta's assistant." Violet dug back into the bag and found a multi-colored scarf in gold and blue and tied it around my head, pirate style. She put her head to one side. "Wait, I think I've got an extra pair of gold hoops. I wasn't sure which size I wanted, so I brought both." She was already wearing enormous gold earrings. I couldn't imagine what the rejects looked like, but as it turned out, they were smaller. More like the width of a cardboard toilet roll tube, unlike Violet's, which looked big enough that hamsters could use them as exercise wheels.

Once I'd put on the earrings and Vi had added a pound or two of makeup to my face, giving me dramatically painted eyes and red, red lips, she stood back and surveyed me critically. "That will have to do."

My job was to stand outside the tent, put people's names on a list, take their money, and usher them in when Madame Violetta was ready for them. It seemed simple enough. I doubted I could screw it up.

Even though the fair didn't start for another half hour, cars were already arriving, disgorging families with excited kids of all ages.

A second, smaller patio table sat outside the tent, and on it was a pad of paper and pen suitable for making lists. There was even a plastic chair for me to sit on and a metal money box that locked. All the proceeds of the fête were going to support a maintenance project on the bell tower of the old church.

Violet retreated back into the tent while I prepared a rudimentary schedule, marking out times and spaces for names. Violet felt she could do a reading in ten minutes, so I blocked out twelve-minute slots to give a bit of breathing room. While I was doing this, an officious-looking woman came up. She checked her clipboard, then looked at me. "Tent number thirty-two? Fortunes by Violetta?" I nodded and pointed up at Theodore's sign.

The woman gazed up at it and sniffed. "A bit over the top, isn't it?"

I disliked her on sight. She had a sharp nose and a pinched-looking, humorless mouth, as though life consistently gave her lemons and instead of making lemonade, she sucked them. She wore a bright pink sun hat with plastic flowers on it, a yellow T-shirt and a flowered cotton skirt—and she thought our sign was over the top? Still, I gave the woman my best smile, as the badge pinned to her shirt said she was Hilary Beaumont, the fête coordinator. "Well, it's all in aid of charity, isn't it?"

With another sniff, the woman moved on.

When the fête opened at eleven, we already had two clients

signed up to see Madame Violetta. Obviously friends, they looked to be in their early thirties. The redhead said, "I came last year, and she was ever so good, the fortune-teller. She said I was going to have a boy, and I did. Little Justin." Using her hand to indicate a pregnant belly, she said, "I was out to here, and everyone said it was going to be a girl, but Madame Tatania, she knew."

I imagined Madame Tatania had reckoned on a fifty percent chance of being right, but all I said was, "Unfortunately, Madame Tatania isn't here this year. We're very excited to have Madame Violetta with us instead."

The woman looked disappointed. "Oh, is she as good, then?"

"I've heard she's excellent." I wasn't lying. I'd heard it from Madame Violetta herself. From the depths of the tent, a heavy female voice sounded like a cross between a heavy-smoking Frenchman, a Russian countess and a Jersey girl. "Let the first person come in."

I told little Justin's mother to go ahead. Her friend said, "It's very exciting, isn't it? Being able to predict the future? I've got two dates this week. I'm hoping she'll tell me that one of them is my soul mate."

"I hope so, too."

Ten minutes went by, and little Justin's mother came running out, tears pouring down her face. Her friend looked startled. "Jeannie, what's wrong?"

Her friend waved her away and ran away from the village green and toward the public toilets. Her friend looked at me, puzzled. "Should I go after her?"

Madame Violetta boomed out, "I am ready to tell ze next fortune."

"Why don't you go on in? I'm sure your friend will be fine."

Three more women came up, and I added their names to the list.

Everyone was in a good mood, giggling and gossiping. The second woman stumbled out of the dark tent and blinked as she emerged into the bright sunlight, as though unsure of her footing. I said, brightly, "Did she tell you whether one of your dates this week will be the one?"

The woman looked at me, stunned. "No. She said they're both losers and I should stop wasting my time with online dating. She says I need to work on my inner insecurities before anyone will fancy me."

"I'm sure she didn't mean—"

"I have to find my friend. I wonder if it's too early to go to the pub."

CHAPTER 3

I'd have gone after her, but a well-dressed older couple arrived. They were probably in their late sixties and looked like a comfortable retired couple. She wore a yellow cotton dress and a large sun hat, and he had on beige cotton trousers and a blue cardigan sweater over a blue and white checked shirt. "Did you both want to see Madame Violetta?"

The woman laughed. "No. It's just me. Harry thinks psychics are nonsense." I took her two pounds and ushered her into the tent.

Her husband hovered as though not sure where to go while his wife was busy.

I now knew enough about knitting that I could say to him, "That's a lovely cardigan. Did your wife knit it for you?"

He turned to me and studied my face as though he might later be asked to draw it. Then his eyes narrowed as he chuckled. "How are you so sure I didn't knit it myself?"

"Perhaps you did. I know plenty of men who knit." Some of them were even undead. It wasn't that I believed knitting was only for women, more that this man didn't seem like the knitting type.

"In fact, your guess was correct. My wife's a champion knitter," he said with pride. "Well, she had to be. I left her alone so often in my working life, you see. I was a police officer."

I knew from my brief time dating Detective Inspector Ian Chisholm how true that was. I wondered how any of them got married, given that they were so often on call. Or perhaps that was just the detectives. I glanced around me at the happy people enjoying a village fair in the sunshine. I suspected that the greatest crime committed today would be not putting on enough sunscreen. "Was this your beat?" I asked.

He shook his head. "I was stationed in Oxford, though I did spend a few weeks here once on a case. I think that's when I fell in love with the place." His brow furrowed. "Even though we never did solve the case." He rocked back on his heels, and I felt that he was looking into the past. "It was a nasty business. A murder."

"A murder? Here?"

His eyes were a faded green, like a cloth napkin that had once been the color of grass but repeated washings had muted it to a pale sage. He had the air of command about him, and I suspected that whatever he'd done, he'd ended up in charge. His eyes were wise and a little sad. "Don't be fooled by these charming little English villages. They all hide secrets. The way a smiling face can hide dark thoughts, so does the glowing Cotswold stone hide some terrible deeds."

Sadly, I knew he was right. Still, it was a beautiful sunny day, and I believed everyone was here today to have a good time.

However, my cousin Violet lived here. Great-Aunt Lavinia didn't live far away, and even Margaret Twig resided in the vicinity. "If they never caught the murderer, do you think there's any danger to the people who live here now?"

He shook his head. "I shouldn't think so. Well, I moved here with my wife, so clearly I think it's a safe village. It was an odd case, that. Grayson Timmins was a pillar of the community. No debts, no scandal, went to church regularly. He was killed in his own home. It looked as though he interrupted a burglary. People said it was a random act. An outsider who came to town, was caught in the act of robbing the house and killed the owner, who'd surprised him."

That sounded plausible to me. "And you didn't believe that?"

He glanced at the tent, but his wife was obviously still occupied. "Do you ever get an instinct? An inexplicable sense about something?"

I nodded, probably more enthusiastically than he was expecting.

Once more his eyes crinkled in a smile. "My wife told you that I don't believe in psychics or any of that nonsense, and it's true, but when you've been a copper for enough years, you develop an instinct. Mine was that it wasn't a random burglar who killed that man."

I saw a shadow cross his face. "You thought you knew who did it, didn't you?"

His body jerked in surprise. "You're a very astute young woman. Yes. I did." He shook his head. "But a man can't be in two places at once." He rocked back and forth again. "In the end, we had to move on. Of course, the case remains open. I still hope that one day someone will come forward or new evidence will present itself." He shrugged. "In the meantime, I play golf, do a bit of gardening, and drive my wife regularly to Yorkshire to see the grandchildren and her mother, who hasn't been too well. She's over ninety and takes great pride in still living alone. Still, we like to get up as often as we can and keep an eye on her."

I smiled at his slightly petulant tone. "It sounds like a nice life."

"It is. Just a bit boring." I laughed, and he said, "You should think about joining the police force. You've got a way about you that makes a person say more than they intended to."

I'd already had more to do with crime than I needed in one lifetime. "I'm very happy running a knitting shop. I have all the respect in the world for the police, but I couldn't do that work."

"A knitting shop? Not in this town, surely?"

"No. In Oxford."

"That lovely little shop on Harrington Street?"

I chuckled. "The very one. Cardinal Woolsey's."

"Oh, my dear, my wife loves your shop. It's where most of my policeman's pension goes, I can tell you."

Since I was pretty sure he was joking, I laughed as though it were a good joke. He said, "You may laugh, but I can never get over that it costs more money for her to knit a jumper herself than it would to buy one brand new at a John Lewis department store."

I gave him the same argument I gave every husband who complained about prices. "Those are knit by machine. The beauty of a hand-knitted sweater is all the love and care that goes into it. No two are ever exactly alike."

"Yes, that's what my wife always says. But she likes to keep her hands busy, and she tells me she finds it soothing."

I would have found some bland answer to that, as I always did, since I could never see what was soothing about knitting. To me, it was a fiendish activity full of tangles and frustration resulting in a soreness that I got between my shoulder blades. I was spared answering, however, when his wife emerged from the tent. Because of the large hat, I didn't immediately see her face, but her husband, the former policeman, did. He took two quick steps forward. "Emily, whatever's wrong?"

Now that I looked at her under the brim of her hat, I could

see that her face was deathly pale and her eyes wide. "She says Mum won't live the summer out. She's got advanced cancer and won't tell any of us because she thinks we'll put her in a home." She glanced around blindly. "Harry, take me home and let's pack. I want to be on the road by tomorrow."

"Emily," he said in a comforting tone. "She's an amateur psychic at a village fair. No doubt you somehow let slip that you have an aged mother, and she took an educated guess."

"She didn't say Mum will die within the year, she said she's dying now, of cancer. I can't take the chance that she might be right. We have to go."

Since her voice rose at the end with a quiver that suggested she was close to tears, her husband said, "Let's go across the road for a nice cup of tea. We'll phone your mother and see how she's faring. I'm sure everything's fine."

He glanced at me then, but I think both of us knew he'd very soon be on the road to visit his mother-in-law.

I was about to have a word with Madame Violetta when an anxious-looking woman of about seventy wearing an old-fashioned house dress with knee socks and sandals walked up. Seeing no line, she said, "Is the psychic free now?"

"Yes." Her name was Dierdre Gunn. I took her two pounds and ushered her in.

A plump, blond woman of about fifty arrived with a dark-haired friend about the same age. She paid her two pounds and said, "I know it's just a bit of fun, but it's for a good cause."

She looked so happy, I almost warned her to be wary, but then I thought Violet couldn't come up with too many bad fortunes in a row. It would be like tossing coins and getting heads turn up endlessly, if heads were bad news.

I put their names on the list. The blonde was Elizabeth Palmer and her friend, Nora Betts.

While they waited their turn, they chatted to each other and to me. Elizabeth said, "I had such fun at the white elephant. Usually, it's a bunch of rubbish, but there were some good things there this year."

I thought of the poodle lamp and reminded myself that everyone's taste was different. Fortunately, the brown paper bag she was carrying was too small for a lamp. She saw me looking. "It's for my husband. He's always wanted a pocket watch." She drew out a round silver watch on a chain. The case featured an interesting design engraved on it, sort of like a vine of grape leaves. How was it some customers found gorgeous watches and I got caught up by kitsch? "It's for our silver wedding anniversary, you see. I'm ever so pleased with it. Of course, it was a bit more expensive than most of the items there, but it's all for a good cause, and this was really a bargain. It's sterling silver. You can see the hallmarks." She showed me the four small symbols stamped into the watch. They certainly looked like sterling hallmarks, not that I was any expert. She obviously didn't think I knew much, either, so she pointed to the lion with a raised paw stamped into the back of the watch case. "That means it's British sterling." Then she pointed to an anchor symbol. "I think that means it was registered in Birmingham. The next one is a date stamp, but I'm not sure what a 'D' means. This is clearly an old watch, though. And then the DE is the mark of the watchmaker. No idea who he was," she finished cheerfully.

"Wow. You know a lot about silver."

"Not really. My husband's interested, so he shows me watches in antique shops that are always too pricey for us to afford. I guess all that looking finally paid off."

"Does the watch keep time?" I asked, more, I think, for something to say than that I really cared.

"Yes, quite well." And she snapped open the case. The watch was, indeed, keeping perfect time, as I could tell since my mobile phone showed the same time.

"It was an excellent buy," her friend Nora said. "Jason will be so pleased."

Violet's most recent customer emerged from the tent and blinked as though unaccustomed to sunlight.

"Next," came the deep tones of Madame Violetta, and I ushered in Elizabeth with a quick, "Good luck."

"Excuse me," I said to her friend and followed Violet's last customer, who had gone about twenty steps and was now leaning on a tree as though she needed the support.

"Mrs. Gunn? Is everything all right?" I asked.

She blinked and then focused on my face. "Oh, it's you. You're the assistant."

"Yes. I hope Madame Violetta didn't give you bad news?" Though it was written all over the woman's stricken countenance that she had.

"She told me that Billy's going to die."

Billy wasn't the only one who was going to die if I had to put up with much more of this. "I'm so sorry. Is that your husband? Son?"

"Billy's my budgie. He's been with me six years now. He's off his food a bit and hasn't been so lively, but he's young yet for a bird." She sounded so sorrowful I could hardly bear it.

I said, "Madame Violetta is only someone from the community who's filling in for Madame Tatania. I doubt she's very good. Honestly, I think she's making things up."

She nodded. "Well, it's a mean trick if she is. I'll go home right now and check on poor Billy."

As she hurried across the road, I tried to think of a spell to prolong bird life. I drew a blank, but I seriously wished Billy a long and happy life.

I returned to my post and added three more people to the list. We were now booked an hour ahead. Vi would be pleased.

We had quite a long line of people waiting when the

formerly cheerful-looking Elizabeth Palmer stumbled out. My heart sank. "Did she tell you something good?"

She looked as though she were coming from a funeral, not a fun little fortune-telling. "She said I mustn't cross water or I'll die." The woman put both hands to her chest. "It's our twenty-fifth wedding anniversary next month. We're going on a cruise." And then she burst into tears.

I felt terrible to be standing outside this tent of misery, taking people's money. "Look, Madame Violetta isn't really a fortune-teller. Please don't let her spoil your day. Would you like your two pounds back?"

She waved my offer away. "I need to talk to my husband. I wonder if it's too late to cancel our trip."

I put on what I hoped was a soothing fortune-teller's assistant's smile and said to the line of frightened-looking people, "Excuse me for one moment." And I slipped into the tent. Violet was adjusting the scarf around the fishbowl when I came in. I glared at her. "What are you doing to these people?"

She looked up at me in surprise. "I'm telling them what I see in their futures. That's what fortune-tellers do."

I shook my head so hard the silk scarf slid down over one ear. "No. It is not what fortune-tellers do. Especially not in a village fair. They tell single women they'll meet a tall, handsome stranger. They tell anxious-looking folks that they're going to get good news very soon. You'll go on a journey across the sea is another common fortune. You got that right, but you don't tell the punters that they'll die when they get to the other side." My voice had started to rise, so I quieted down so as not to alarm the waiting customers more than they already had been.

Violet seemed to be growing quite comfortable in her new role as Madame Violetta. She settled back in her plastic lawn chair and put her arms out, waving her palms over the upside-down fishbowl. "I must be true to my art."

"Violet, that woman is thinking about canceling her twenty-fifth anniversary cruise with her husband. All because you told her that if she crosses water she'll die."

Violet looked relieved. "I'm glad. She should cancel that trip. Honestly, Lucy, I saw death and water in her future."

I felt uncomfortable. "Really?"

"Yes."

"And what about those other poor women? The one who only wanted to see if she'd find a good date, the one who now thinks her mother has cancer and the lady whose bird is going to die?"

Violet made a dismissive motion. "The first one has low self-esteem and terrible taste in men. I told her she needs to work on that. That's positive, right? That woman's mother is in the last stages of cancer. And that bird *is* going to die. Probably today."

"I don't think you're quite getting this fortune-teller thing. For a couple of quid, all they want is something mysterious and exciting in their future. The single ones want to think an attractive man will come into their lives, and the married ones want to come into money. Mothers want to hear that their children will be successful and famous. People who hate their jobs want to be told they're about to win the lottery. And nobody wants to know that their beloved pet is going to die."

She looked petulant. "All right. But I'm not telling any lies."

"You don't have to. Everyone must have something good in their future that you can see. Just keep the bad stuff to yourself."

"Fine. But I did see death and water in that woman's future."

I put my hands on my hips. "How specific was your vision? Maybe she'll live to be ninety-five and drown in the bathtub. Do you really want her to spend the next forty or fifty years terrified to set foot on a boat?"

She adjusted her turban. "No."

"If you want me to continue as your assistant, you need to start giving out brighter fortunes."

She glared at me. "You're awfully bossy for an assistant."

I raised my eyebrows at her. "I wonder where I got that notion from."

CHAPTER 4

*W*hen I came back outside the tent, Nora, the friend of the woman who was going to die if she crossed water, was nibbling her lip and looking toward the center of the village green. "She's so upset. She said to leave her alone, but I wonder if I should skip my fortune and go after her?"

In a soothing tone, I said, "You go in and have your reading. I'll go and talk to her." And then I dropped my voice to a near whisper and assured her that Madame Violetta had already indicated the person waiting outside was going to get some good news. In fact, I was positive that from now on, every customer was going to receive a good fortune.

She nodded, looking relieved, and then walked into the tent. I knew I had at least fifteen minutes before I needed to be back.

I told the next person in line that I was just going to refresh my water bottle, which, in fact, I did need to do, and that I'd be back before it was her turn. The people in line nearly all knew one another and were happily chatting away as I left.

Violet was always telling me I needed to work on my craft, and this was a perfect opportunity to practice a forgetting spell. If I could get Elizabeth alone for a minute, I was fairly certain I could erase in about two minutes the damage my cousin Violet had done.

I practiced the forgetting spell in my head.

I went around the corner of the tent and looked around for Elizabeth Palmer and soon caught a glimpse of her. She had her hand shading her eyes and seemed to be looking for someone. I had a terrible feeling it was her husband or perhaps her travel agent.

I hurried to follow her. With so many people at the fair, she kept disappearing behind family groups and huddles of teenagers pretending this was all beneath them. There was a sudden crash of drums. I jumped, as I think everyone in the vicinity did. I glanced around and discovered the Forest of Wychwood Pipe and Drum Band was warming up.

The band members had gone all out and were wearing bright red uniforms and tall, black busby hats with gold piping. They looked like the Queen's Guard. One guy in the center banged an enormous drum. It must have been four feet in diameter. He was also on the larger side, probably six-foot-three or four inches, and he drummed with such humorous flourish that people began to laugh and draw near.

I would have loved to go and watch, but I was conscious of the time. I needed to find Elizabeth, wipe her bad fortune from her mind, then refill my water bottle before Violet was ready for her next client.

I glanced around, looking for the blond woman. I couldn't immediately see her and, as she had done, I shaded my eyes with my hand and scanned the area ahead of me.

I began walking in the general direction I thought she had taken when suddenly I heard a scream. Even over the noise of the pipe band, the sound carried, high-pitched and terrible.

I began to run toward the sound. I wasn't the only one. From all sides, those of us who'd heard the wail of panic and despair heeded the call.

Now I could see the screamer. Tall, thin and blond, she windmilled her arms. "Help me. Help me!"

I sprinted across the grass and heard the hollow knocking sound as my shoes hit the wooden bridge over the stream. On the other side, as my feet hit grass, I came to a halt.

I could see now why that woman was screaming. The poor woman who had been ready to celebrate her twenty-fifth wedding anniversary would not be going on her cruise after all. Her life's journey was over. She lay on her back, her sightless eyes staring up at the cloudless sky.

An arrow was sticking out of her chest.

A man I didn't know fell to his knees by her side and checked her pulse. He glanced up and shook his head. "She's dead."

The woman who'd been screaming initially screamed even louder now. The pipe band played on, heedlessly, and in the distance, I could hear the occasional thwack of arrows hitting the targets at the archery field. Across the way, Punch was fighting with Judy and children were laughing.

But around the dead woman was a circle of hushed silence and, as more people began to realize what was going on, that circle spread like ripples in a pond after a heavy stone has been thrown into it.

I couldn't seem to think. My head was buzzing. She'd been so alive only minutes ago. How I wished that Violet hadn't given her that stupid fortune or I had caught up to her more quickly. I was so sad that this poor woman had ended her life worried that she would die if she crossed water.

Then, with a horrified shiver, I realized that she had walked across the wooden bridge over the stream and, almost as soon as she reached the other side, she'd been struck by that arrow.

Violet had been right. She had crossed water, and then she had died.

CHAPTER 5

*a*s more and more people became aware of the tragedy, the fête acted like a body dying of frostbite. It froze bit by bit, leaving the inner organs for last.

So the archers dropped their bows as soon as they realized what had happened. The play area shut down as mothers and fathers rushed to gather up their children. People left their tents to gather around. The last areas to finally cease functioning were the marching band, the Punch and Judy, and the pie stall.

As an unnatural hush spread over the fairgrounds, it was disconcerting to hear a band playing military marching songs. The song petered out in mid-march, so I could hear the screeches of laughter from the children sitting watching the Punch and Judy show, and then, finally, all I heard was calls for "steak and kidney, mushroom and vegetable, curried chicken, lovely home-baked pies! Come and get 'em while they're hot!" And then, from the same voice, "What? Blimey!" And even the cries from the pie seller ceased.

I waited by the body, not because I knew this poor woman, but in case the police needed me. I imagined Detective

Inspector Ian Chisholm would soon show up. He'd known me for a while now, and he could trust me to tell him the truth and to give my observations in a coherent manner.

The officious Hilary Beaumont, the fête coordinator, came rushing up, red in the face, her eyes bulging as though it were an outrage that something so dreadful should happen on her watch. When she'd confirmed that there was, indeed, a dead woman in the middle of the village green, she cried, "Oh, whatever shall we do? Whatever shall we do?"

Her hysteria began to infect others. I decided to set her a task so she could do something more useful than panic. "Find some people you trust to form a perimeter to stop people coming closer. The children shouldn't see this."

"But the police?"

"We won't disturb the body."

She nodded and ran away. I had thought she might try to assert her authority, but she was too happy to get away from the sight of death to argue with me. Within minutes, a ring of adult men and women were creating a ragged circle and stopping any more people joining the crowd.

I didn't know much about death, but I suspected from the little blood that had come out of the wound that Elizabeth Palmer's end must've been very quick.

While we waited for the police, I could see parents gathering up their children and beginning to walk home or head to cars. I looked around for the organizer and saw her talking in urgent tones with the woman who ran the white elephant sale.

I didn't need my acute hearing to make a pretty good guess at the subject. I willed Hilary Beaumont to look at me, and when she did, I beckoned her over. Reluctantly she came close enough that I could say, "You've got to stop people leaving. The police will be here soon, and they'll want to interview everyone."

As her shock ebbed, her officiousness returned. She held

her clipboard as though it were a badge of office. "Who put you in charge? You're just the fortune-teller's assistant."

I held on to my patience the way a toddler holds on to a balloon. With slack fingers. I could feel my control sliding away from me. I said, with forced calm, "You must know I'm right. At the very least, you need to get names and phone numbers of everyone who was here when this woman was tragically killed."

Fortunately, her friend from the white elephant came forward. "Oh, poor Elizabeth. What a terrible thing. My goodness, yes. We'd better start with the archery people. One of the archers must have accidentally turned around just as the arrow was about to go off. We've never had anything like this in the forty years we've been running this village fête."

She glanced around and told Hilary Beaumont that they'd need to get the rest of the fête committee to help them. She seemed to have the matter well in hand, and Hilary listened to her without arguing.

A Range Rover with tinted windows drove slowly past and stopped behind the archery area. I thought for a moment it was the police, but no one got out of the car. There was no siren. It was as quiet and evasive as a creature of the night. And even as I had that thought, a chill went down the back of my neck. I immediately realized who it was.

Rafe Crosyer was a five-hundred-year-old vampire with an uncanny ability to find me, especially when there was trouble afoot.

I didn't completely understand how the vampires managed to get about in daylight. Since I'd arrived in the winter and it was so frequently cloudy in Oxford, I'd often seen Rafe out walking the streets in the daytime, though usually it was early in the morning or in the afternoon and evening. But since the weather had turned bright and sunny, I was seeing much less of my vampires during the day. If they were out, they tended to wear large sun hats or carry umbrellas made of technical fabric that shielded them from UV rays.

I tried to ignore the black vehicle, which was easy as I now heard the sound of sirens approaching. People around me began to stand up straighter and appear more serious or suddenly engage in some activity as though they'd been standing around and a stage director had called "action."

I didn't move. I remained at my post beside the dead woman. I was soon joined by the man who ran the archery. His name was Hubert Drosselmeyer. He was enormous and blond and it was easy to imagine him as a medieval archer heading into battle with his longbow. He looked concerned, verging on panicked. When he looked down at the dead woman with the arrow in her, he shook his head. "I don't understand. It's impossible for such an accident to happen."

I was tempted to ask questions, but I knew I would be stepping on Ian's toes and he wouldn't appreciate it. However, by keeping quiet, I learned quite a bit. The man seemed desperate to talk about his dilemma, and, even without asking questions and merely looking silently sympathetic, he unburdened himself to me.

"We're very strict. We don't just give the punters a bow and arrow and let them shoot at anything. The first thing we talk about is safety. The targets are set up against straw bales." He looked genuinely puzzled, turning his head in the direction of the now-silent archery field and back to the dead woman. "You'd have to be an extremely good archer to hit that woman in the heart from that far away."

"Or extremely unlucky," I said, accidentally breaking my temporary vow of silence. Though, in fairness, I hadn't asked him a question.

He looked as though he were the unlucky one.

An ambulance arrived with a paramedic team and a doctor who, after a brief examination, pronounced her dead. They didn't move her, though, and soon a guy who appeared to be in his mid-thirties and had the bearing and short hair of someone in the military walked up to join them. With him were two uniformed police officers.

It wasn't until he introduced himself as Detective Inspector Thomas that I realized Ian wasn't coming. For some reason I thought that every time there was a homicide, Ian would attend, but that was nonsense, of course. There were other detectives in the area. He turned to the two of us on either side of Elizabeth Palmer's body. "Did either of you see what happened?"

Hubert Drosselmeyer shook his head. "I never saw anything. Someone said there was a woman killed by an arrow, but I didn't believe it until I saw her for myself."

The detective turned to me with his eyebrows raised.

"I was walking this way when I heard a scream. I must have arrived within a minute, but she was dead."

He nodded. "See who shot her?"

I flinched. "It all happened so fast. There was a blond woman screaming when I arrived, but I think someone led her to the first aid van."

More cops arrived, and they put tenting around the body to shield it from public scrutiny. DI Thomas told the uniformed cops to interview everyone who was still at the fête and find out if they'd seen anything and to make sure they got every single person's name, their phone number, their address and what they'd been doing at the time of the tragedy.

Perhaps because we'd been beside the body when the police arrived, they didn't move me and Hubert right away. It was as though we'd been grandfathered in to this tragedy. I looked once more at that round face, still wearing the look of shocked surprise. But Hubert squinted at her chest and the arrow still protruding. He said, with enormous relief in his tone, "Wait. That arrow's not one of ours."

All of us stared at his face. DI Thomas said, "Are you sure?"

He nodded emphatically. "Come to the archery area and I can show you. We use short bows similar to what they'd have used in medieval times. Our own in-house fletcher makes them, and the ones we use for practice and displays like this one all have a blue and red feather on the end of the shaft." We could all see that the feather thing on this arrow was black.

He was gaining confidence now. He moved to the side of the body, got to his hands and knees and squinted. "I've been an archer for twenty years. I'm sure your medical examiner will back me up on this, but that arrow could never have been fired from the archery pitch. Look at the angle of the arrow's entry."

Now all of us squatted down on our haunches and bent our heads so that we could see what he was referring to. I understood what he meant. The arrow wasn't sticking straight out. It was on an angle. I spoke my thoughts aloud. "It looks as though it came from above and hit her."

He nodded, looking at me in approval. "That's exactly what happened. If it was deliberate, it was an excellent shot."

A shiver ran down my spine. "You're saying this might not have been an accident?"

He was getting some color back in his face. "What kind of fool would be up a tree or in one of the buildings overlooking the village green with a bow and arrow and shoot it into a crowd? No, it was murder. The only question in my mind is whether it was a random act or whether this woman was deliberately targeted for murder."

CHAPTER 6

*N*ora and Violet came running up at that moment. I imagined they'd been so busy in the fortune-telling booth they hadn't heard the commotion. Until now.

Nora pushed passed the onlookers and cried out, "Elizabeth. No!"

Violet looked at me and then at the stream, and as the color drained from her face, her makeup stood out like a bizarre mask.

"How could this happen?" Nora cried.

"There, there, love," the woman from the white elephant said, taking her into her arms.

Hubert Drosselmeyer said, "The arrow entered at about a forty-degree angle." He looked down at Elizabeth Palmer, who was still staring up. I wished someone would close her eyes. "How tall was she?"

Okay, I had to pull myself together and try to help. I'd stood talking to her. "I think she was about my height."

"Good." The archer rose and turned me so my back was to him. He pulled me against him. "Place your wrist at the level of your heart, with your hand and fingers facing forward."

37

I did.

He reached around and tilted my hand to the same angle as the arrow. I could feel everyone in the crowd watching us. He turned my body slightly. "There." And then he pointed up—across the street to where a row of old houses stared back at us. Many of the second- and third-story windows were open on this warm day. He said in a hard voice, "That building in the middle is the village hall, and upstairs we have a museum."

I followed his gaze, and sure enough, the upstairs window was open. "You think the arrow was fired from there?"

"The hall was unlocked for the day. It's where we all stored extra equipment and coats and things. Anyone could have crept in when it was empty and stationed themselves upstairs with a bow and arrow."

I felt a cold chill as I looked up at that window. "But why?" I whispered.

DI Thomas said, "Thank you, sir. You've been very helpful." He made a motion with his chin, and two of the uniforms ran toward the village hall.

Hubert stepped away from me. He said, "The person you're looking for is an excellent shot."

"Such as yourself? Or one of the archers putting on this little display?"

Hubert stood straighter. "I can vouch for everyone who was here today. The mission of the Wychwood Bowmen is to promote healthy enjoyment of this ancient sport. We are not killers."

"I'll ask all of you to remain behind to help us with our enquiries." DI Thomas looked at the rest of us and raised his voice. "Now, if everyone would give their names and contact details to one of our officers and let them know if you saw anything that might help us with our enquiries, you can all go home."

The last thing I wanted to do was stay here. It was too sad. Besides, I needed to talk to Violet. What had she really seen?

I turned to find her and to my consternation discovered that Margaret Twig had turned up. She wore a red and black flowing kaftan over black cotton trousers and a necklace of red beads. Her hair was its usual mass of salt and pepper corkscrew curls.

When I joined her and Violet, she said, "Let's get Violet's belongings out of that tent and get out of here."

I nodded. We gave our names and contact information to one of the uniforms and then headed back to the fortune-teller's tent. The silk banner seemed garish now and out of place on this day of death.

When we were all inside the tent, I said, "But this is such a peaceful, lovely little village. Why would anyone want to murder Elizabeth Palmer?"

Violet said, "Well, it could hardly have been an accident. Someone deliberately killed that woman."

Margaret Twig had no time for all this speculating. She looked seriously annoyed, as she often did when I was around. "There is no such thing as a quiet, peaceful village. Whenever more than two people gather together, there will always be secrets, intrigues, and scandal. The English village is like a microcosm of the whole world. On the outside you see the tumble of pretty cottages with their climbing roses and Union Jack bunting, but inside there's as much darkness, rage and hate as you'll find anywhere. You forget that at your peril."

"But the death happened at the village fair. A celebration of everything that's good about small villages in England."

Margaret and my cousin exchanged a glance. Margaret continued, "There have been witches in Moreton-under-Wychwood for centuries. The locals have always known it in the way you can know that an underground river runs beneath your

39

property without ever having to see it. So long as it doesn't flood your house and destroy your land, you're quite happy to let that river flow in peace. But the minute you get water up around your ankles, you will dam that river, reroute it or dry it up in any way you can."

I found this a rather confusing metaphor. "You're saying that we witches are like an underground river?"

"Exactly. So long as we stay out of sight and mind our own business, the people of Moreton-Under-Wychwood have always turned a blind eye. Most of them are clever enough to know that we do good here. We help with the harvest, and long before there were proper doctors and hospitals, it was the wise women who helped with the pains of childbirth, cured the sick and tried our best to keep out the forces of evil."

Violet nodded. "And now, it looks as though some kind of evil is at work."

My eyes widened. "You think that woman was killed by some malevolent supernatural being?"

Margaret turned a pointed, bright-blue gaze my way. "You're awfully friendly with that nest of vampires who live in the tunnels underneath your shop. Maybe you should ask them."

Anger began to burn in my belly. "Don't you suggest for one minute that they had anything to do with this. You're only doing to vampires what humans have been doing to witches for centuries. Blaming them for the inexplicable. You should know better."

Clearly she didn't take kindly to my rebuking her, but I didn't care. I stood glaring at her, feeling my chest rise and fall rapidly with anger.

"Prove it was human killing human, and I'll take your vampire friends off my most-wanted list."

"They weren't even here. What self-respecting vampire goes to a village fête on a sunny day in early June?"

Her thin eyebrows rose. "Are you truly that naïve? A Range Rover with tinted glass was parked on the other side of the green. You must know who that belongs to."

Crap. Why had Rafe followed me here? We seriously needed to have a conversation where I explained the difference between friend and stalker.

I looked at the two of them. "You both live around here. Tell me what you know about the dead woman, Elizabeth Palmer. All I know is that she was excited about her twenty-fifth wedding anniversary. She and her husband were planning a cruise. And then Violet told her if she crossed water, she would die."

Violet nodded her head vigorously. "And if she'd listened to me, she might still be alive. Not ten minutes after I warned her, she was walking over a flipping stream." She threw up her hands. "It's like I told her to stay away from fire and she walked straight into a burning building. What is the point of telling fortunes if people ignore you?"

I shook my head. "I don't think she even thought of crossing that little stream as going over water. I'm sure she thought that you meant an ocean voyage."

"I didn't say ocean voyage, did I?"

Well, she learned her lesson.

Margaret Twig said, "Snapping at each other won't get us anywhere. Here's what I know about the dead woman. Her husband runs a car dealership. It used to be her father's. Twenty-five years or, I suppose, twenty-six years ago now, he came to work for her father as a salesman. That's how Elizabeth and Jason met. The gossip around the village was that her parents strongly disapproved of the match, but it was the mid-1990s, not the 1950s, so there wasn't much they could do about it. Elizabeth got her way, and she and Jason were married. When her father died, he took over the family business. They lived in the big house with her mother until she, too, died, and that came to Elizabeth and Jason as well."

I said, "They must've been proven wrong. The marriage had clearly lasted, and the couple must have been happy if they were planning an anniversary cruise."

"I don't come into town all that often, but I'm fairly certain that they were quite good friends with another couple about their own age. Nora and Tony Betts."

I nodded. "Nora Betts and she were in line together waiting to have their fortunes read. They seemed to be best friends."

I glanced at Violet. "Remember, Violet? After you told the woman she'd die if she crossed water, her friend came in. Do you remember what you told her?"

Violet sniffed. "Was that after you gave me a lecture and told me I couldn't tell my paying customers the truth? That I had to make up some nonsense about meeting handsome strangers and coming into money?"

I rolled my eyes. "Yes. After I told you to stop terrifying the customers so they came running out of your tent in tears."

She seemed very pleased with herself. "I did exactly what you told me to. I told her she'd come into some money."

"But what did you really see?"

"I told you I wasn't going to lie, and I didn't. She will come into money."

"A lot of money?"

She closed her eyes as though casting herself back. "I saw a hand writing out a check. It was in the hundreds of thousands of pounds."

"I call that a lot of money. Any idea where it came from?"

"I'm a fortune-teller, not a forensic accountant."

"Violet," I reminded her, "you are a witch. Think carefully. Did you see anything else in your vision?"

"It was a man's hand signing the check. I could see the edge of a shirt cuff and the sleeve of a business-suit jacket. Then the screaming started, and I lost the vision."

"Well, it's a lead. One of the most common motives for murder is financial gain. Is there some way Nora might come into money when Elizabeth died? Maybe her friend left her something in her will?" I thought back to the two women giggling together the way best friends do. "She'd have to be pretty cold-blooded to be joking around with her friend, knowing she was about to murder her."

"She couldn't have done it without help, obviously, since she was with me when her friend was killed."

I was thinking. I said, "Violet, what if you and I went together to commiserate on her loss?"

"But we don't know her."

She was right. "Okay, what about this? You saw something else in your fortune that you didn't tell her."

"But I didn't see anything else."

"Sometimes, we have to stretch the truth in the name of justice. We won't tell her anything that could change her life. Just something that would make her feel better on this very dark and sad day when she's lost her friend."

"Like what?"

"I don't know." I looked at Margaret Twig. "What kind of news would you like to get from a stranger?"

"Finding out I was going to be several hundred thousand pounds richer would be all the news I needed."

I thought for a minute. "Why don't we do what lots of fake fortune-tellers do? We'll ask around, find out more about this woman. Everyone's gossiping about the murder anyway. They're bound to talk about these two friends. We'll find out things about her, like what her job is, where her home is, if she has children and what they're like. If her pride and joy is her family, we'll tell her that her child is going to win a school prize or something. Or her prize dog is going to win a championship."

Margaret looked as though she were tasting something bitter. "Dogs. Nasty, smelly little beasts. If young enough, though, they're very good in a potion to make sure a pregnant woman gives birth to a boy."

"Margaret!" I said, shocked.

Her superior smile bloomed, wicked and taunting. "Where do you think that rhyme came from that says boys are made of slugs and snails and puppy dog tails?"

"But that's revolting. Please tell me you've never—"

She broke into her evil cackle. "Really, Lucy, with you, it's too easy."

She might be teasing me, but I would be very careful not to let any puppies get near Margaret Twig. "Where is gossip central in this town?"

Violet said, "Well, there's the coffee shop and the pub. And pretty much anywhere two people in this small town meet, they end up chatting to each other. There's not much else to do."

"Right. I think you and I should head to the pub. I don't know about you, but I could definitely use a drink."

We went in and, as I had expected, the place was packed. No doubt it would've been busy anyway at the end of a village fête, but today all benches and tables in the pub garden were full. When Violet and I went inside the pub, they were standing three deep waiting to be served at the bar and, again, every seat was taken. People were standing in groups talking quietly. The atmosphere was nervous and high-strung.

I said, "Why are people looking at us that way?"

Margaret Twig said in a very low voice, "Because they suspect that Violet and I are witches. You'd do much better if you weren't seen with us, Lucy."

I wanted to talk to the dead woman's friend with Violet, but I decided that could wait for tomorrow. Margaret Twig was right. There was no point having townspeople close up with me if they thought I was associated with witches. Come to think of it, I wasn't thrilled that it was an open secret that there were witches in the area.

I understood what Margaret meant, though. So long as the presence of witches here had been benign, no one much bothered. But, as history had shown, the minute things turned ugly, people liked to point a finger.

CHAPTER 7

*V*iolet phoned me the next morning. Her voice sounded strained and near tears. "Lucy, you've got to help me."

I was enjoying a lazy Sunday morning breakfast and browsing through a magazine while I drank my coffee. At her words, my laziness vanished and I sat bolt upright. "What is it?"

"Somebody threw a rock through my window last night."

I told her how sorry I was, but I didn't see why she was quite so worked up until she explained, "It had written symbols on it."

I started to get a bad feeling about this. "Written symbols? What sort?"

She said, "Margaret Twig recognized them. She said they're to ward away evil spirits and frighten away witches."

"Oh my gosh. I thought you only saw things like that in museums."

"Lucy, can you come over? I think people are on edge because of the murder yesterday."

She was right, of course. Besides, I had been one of the last people to talk to Elizabeth and probably one of the first to arrive after she was killed. I felt a keen interest in finding out what had happened to her and, if possible, helping bring her killer to justice.

Not so long ago I would've gagged at the very idea of murder. But since I'd moved to Oxford, I seemed to be forever getting myself into one murder scrape or another. This one, thank goodness, was nothing to do with me. I'd just been in the wrong place at the wrong time. And, sadly, so had Violet.

I agreed to stop by her house and then suggested that we go for coffee at Moreton-Under-Wychwood. The café would be the best place to pick up gossip. And, perhaps, get some idea of who was so angry at Violet.

I was irked when I arrived at Violet's to find Margaret Twig there. Of course, I should have seen that coming. As the head of the coven, Margaret was the correct person to call, but still, my morning would've been brighter without having to see her. Violet's grandmother, my great aunt Lavinia, was also there. She rushed up to give me a hug when she saw me. "Lucy, what a dreadful thing. I'm terribly worried about Violet. We've never had anything like this in our neighborhood before."

Violet shot her a sideways glance, and she amended, "Well, not in the last century, anyway."

Whatever horror stories of witch persecution had occurred locally, I really didn't want to hear them right now. I was much more interested in present-day murder. I reiterated my plan for Violet and me to go for coffee, ask questions and listen to gossip. To my horror, both Lavinia and Margaret Twig decided to come, too. I didn't know how to tell them they weren't invited, so I made the best of it, and the four of us crammed into my small car and drove into town.

Every seat in the coffee shop was taken and the place was buzzing with chatter, but when we walked in, a sudden hush fell over the crowd. It was awful.

I felt every eye on our little group, and you didn't have to be a witch to feel the animosity flowing toward us.

Violet said in a soft voice, "Maybe we should leave."

"Absolutely not." Margaret was looking feisty and irritable, which seemed like a dangerous attitude in this crowd.

I had to agree that we shouldn't let ourselves be frightened away, but it was somewhat unnerving feeling so much dislike coming from people I didn't even know.

A young couple with two children got up and left their table in the corner. I noticed that they walked around the very outside of the coffee shop rather than take the more direct route past us. I felt as though we were carrying some sort of plague and people were terrified they'd catch it if they got too near us.

We all ordered coffee and then settled around the table, or pretended to settle. Conversation began again, mostly in low voices, and the way my skin prickled, I was certain the topic of conversation was witches.

Peace was barely restored when, suddenly, a woman burst into the café. Oh, dear. It was Dierdre Gunn, the woman whose budgie hadn't been too well. Violet had predicted its demise.

She looked around and then, when she saw Violet, pointed with triumph. I suspected somebody had contacted her on their mobile, as she'd come in already knowing Violet was in the café. She wiggled between tables until she was standing in the middle of the coffee shop. Then she pointed a shaking finger at Violet. "You killed my Billy."

Violet glanced around as though someone might help her, but there was deathly silence. "I didn't."

"You did, you lying witch. He was perfectly healthy when I left for the village fête, and then you looked into your crystal ball. You said some words. I know it was an evil spell, and you said he was going to die. You killed him."

Violet stood up to face her accuser. "He was old. He died of old age."

A new voice entered the fray. The young woman who'd been told she needed to work on her self-esteem stood up and came to stand beside Dierdre Gunn. "And she told me that neither of my dates this week would work out. When I got home, there were two messages canceling dates. She put an evil spell on me, too."

Violet looked stunned at this new accusation. "I told you that you needed to work on your self-esteem and that they were both losers. I never said they were going to cancel on you."

The woman was not mollified. "You've cursed me. You've cursed me so I'll never be lucky in love."

Dierdre Gunn patted her shoulder and said, "There, there, dear. It's not so bad living alone. What you need is a pet." Her lower lip trembled. "Like my Billy." And then she burst into tears.

I didn't know if any of these people would believe witches had put spells on them normally, but people were on edge because of the sudden death at the fair, and mob mentality began to rule.

Violet looked around and then saw Nora, Elizabeth's best friend, sitting in the corner with a man who was presumably her husband. Violet said, "You, in the back. Why don't you tell them what I told you? That you'd come into a lot of money."

But when Nora stood up, it wasn't to reassure people that some of Vi's fortunes were good ones. Instead, she cried, "What do I care about money? My best friend's dead. Why didn't you tell me she was about to be killed so I could have saved her?"

"It doesn't work that way."

"What did you have against Elizabeth? We only went to the fair for bit of fun. Now she's dead. People are saying you killed her."

Violet looked around the table as though we three could

help her, but I couldn't think of a thing to say, and Margaret Twig seemed awfully quiet, too.

"Of course I didn't kill her. Why would I? She seemed like a nice person. I was trying to save her."

No, I willed her silently. *Don't go on. Don't say anything more. Don't say...*

"I told her that if she crossed water she would die. And she did cross water."

"But how did you know? How did you know that she would die if she crossed water?"

"Because I saw a vision!" I kicked Vi's ankle under the table, but it was too late. She'd already blurted out the damning truth.

Several more people jumped up, and one man cried out in a hysterical way. "You see? She admits it. She has visions of death. Oh, we haven't had a black witch here in a long time. But you know what we do to black witches, don't you?"

I felt like we were in the Middle Ages and we three were about to be tried and convicted. Of course, there was real fear among the people of Moreton-Under-Wychwood, but I didn't like the way that fear was turning into anger and blame toward Violet and Margaret. They didn't know me, so I didn't feel suspicion directed at me. Yet.

I rose to my feet, not even knowing what I was going to say. They all looked to me. Of course, I was a stranger in these parts. "My name is Lucy. Elizabeth Palmer was killed by an arrow shot from a building across from the green. If we all cooperate with the police, I believe we can find her killer."

"Don't listen to her," said Dierdre Gunn. "She's in cahoots with the other one. She pretended to be her assistant yesterday. But they're both witches, I can tell."

"How can you tell?" I asked with some scorn. I was sorry that her bird had died, but this was ridiculous. She glanced at me with a kind of triumph, and I saw a gleam in her small, dark eyes that I didn't like the look of. She pulled out an opaque white crystal. It looked like quartz, only it had a slightly yellow tint. I'd never seen anything like it.

She was the one who looked like a witch, heading toward us, holding the crystal as though it were an instrument of torture. "If you're not a witch, you've got nothing to fear. But if you are, this crystal will change color."

Even as I scoffed, I heard Margaret say, in a very low voice, "Don't go near that thing. It will give us away."

So I laughed, scornfully, I hoped, and said, "This is foolishness. Lots of stones change color when you touch them. It doesn't mean anything."

I'd heard of mob mentality, certainly read about it, but never in my wildest dreams had I imagined being at the wrong end of so much suspicion. I did not like the way the people of Moreton-Under-Wychwood were looking at us. Unfortunately, or perhaps fortunately, the table we were sitting at was against the wall. The suspicion and malevolence coming at us from all sides had caused each of us to edge back so our four backs were to the wall. This was too much like facing a firing squad or a witch's trial.

The espresso machine fired a burst of steam that startled me but also brought me back to the reality that we were in a village coffee shop in the heart of England, where they hadn't had a witch trial in centuries. At least, not one I'd ever read about.

There had to be a way to defuse this tension, but I didn't know what it was. I felt like one wrong move or wrong word, and these normally perfectly pleasant villagers might turn violent.

The woman was coming closer to us with the crystal, but the café tables were so jammed together that she was having trouble getting around them.

I was racking my brain for an idea and could feel my fellow

witches doing the same. I thought that Margaret Twig was searching for a spell. If we could all disappear and then cause the villagers to forget we'd ever been here, would that work? Not that I had any idea how to cast such a spell, but I tried to toss the idea up in the air and toward Margaret.

It wasn't Margaret who answered my quiet plea, however. I felt rather than heard the words *stay calm* in my head and looked around to find Liam perched on a stool by the bar. Our gazes met briefly, and then I deliberately looked elsewhere, not wanting to draw attention to the magic hiding in plain sight.

I noticed that every time the woman with the crystal tried to come closer, the path was obliterated. A bag would turn out to be in the way, or someone would shift their chair, blocking her.

Liam.

He couldn't keep her back for much longer, but he gave us a couple of minutes to come up with a plan.

I became aware of a new sensation, like chilled fingers at the back of my neck.

That meant that Rafe Crosyer was in the vicinity. Rafe was an extremely powerful vampire, and I could not see that bringing additional supernatural creatures into this standoff was going to help at all.

I felt more and more alarmed. Before I could figure out what to do, the door opened. But it wasn't Rafe who entered, it was Sylvia, and with her was Clara. Both vampires were older women, but while Sylvia, who'd been a film star in the 1920s, always looked glamorous with her silver-white hair perfectly styled and wearing designer clothes, Clara looked like exactly what she had been in life: a comfortable, grandmotherly woman who loved to sit by the fire and knit. Both set down the umbrellas made with high-tech UV protecting fabric that they used as parasols.

I could see from their quick glances around the room that they'd taken in the situation immediately.

Clara walked forward as though completely unaware of the hostile atmosphere. Where the woman with the crystal was blocked, her path seemed magically clear. In a strong voice that easily carried across the entire café, she said, "Lucy, thank goodness. I've made such a tangle of my knitting, and I knew if I could find you, you would help me. It's always so difficult when your knitting shop is closed, I've nowhere to go. Luckily, Sylvia told me I could find you here."

No one in the world looked less like a vampire than Clara, but I knew her power would be fearsome if called upon. From the cold shivers still running up and down my neck, I knew that Rafe was close by, and if trouble started, he'd be here instantly. He wouldn't care who he hurt if it was to protect me. But my goal, and clearly, that of Sylvia and Clara was to prevent any trouble or, heaven forbid, bloodshed.

Clara could, and had, knitted the most exquisite garments. She was also an expert at crochet and lace. She, like so many of the vampires, had attempted to help me improve my knitting and failed. So the idea of her asking me for help would be hilarious except that it was such a brilliant ruse.

Rising to the occasion, I stepped forward, also pretending I couldn't feel the anger and tension that had been directed toward us four women. "Clara, lovely to see you. Of course, I'd be more than happy to help you." I led her to the table and settled her down beside me. She said, in quite a loud voice, "It's so good for my poor legs to sit down for a moment. Sylvia, dear, order me a cappuccino, will you?"

When Sylvia came over to the table with a cappuccino for Clara and an espresso for her, she said under her breath to the other three witches, "Go, now."

They didn't have to be asked twice. When I looked out the shop window, I could see the Range Rover with tinted glass windows that I now knew belonged to Rafe.

Lavinia and Violet and even Margaret Twig all obeyed

Sylvia's command, and while I held my breath with nervousness, they filed out of the coffee shop.

"Are we just going to let them go?" asked Dierdre, whose bird had died. She suddenly looked very foolish standing there waving her crystal about.

Somehow, Clara and her knitting had brought a sense of normalcy back into the charged atmosphere. Someone called out, "What are you planning to do? Tar and feather them?"

She looked suddenly confused and a bit sad. "I don't know. But Billy shouldn't have died like that."

An older man stood up and put his hand on her shoulder. "Come along, then, Dierdre. I'll get my shovel, and we'll bury old Billy in your garden."

She dropped her chin to her chest and allowed him to lead her out of the coffee shop. As they reached the door, I heard him say, "There's a nice pet shop I know of that's got a good selection of tropical birds. When you're ready, I'll drive you over."

"No one can replace Billy."

"Of course not. As I said, when you're ready."

CHAPTER 8

The door shut behind them, and with it, a little more tension left the coffee shop. Honestly, if this had been the Wild West, and we'd been in a saloon instead of a coffee shop, there'd have been a gunfight by now.

Clara, meanwhile, pulled out a piece of knitting. I nearly burst out laughing, as much from nervousness as amusement, when I recognized it as one of my own pieces that I'd abandoned. I said, with a quiver of amusement, "Yes, that really is a mess." I repeated to her what she'd said to me many a time. "Your tension is too tight for a start." Once I'd said that, and very confidently, too, I ran out of steam. Now what? I had no idea how to fix that mess, which was why I'd given up on it. Inspired, I added, "Why don't you unpick the whole thing and we'll start over."

If we began from the very beginning, I could pretend to teach her what I barely understood myself. And Clara, expert that she was, could pretend to fumble while actually knitting the piece properly. It seemed like a win-win to me.

They strongly disapproved, my vampires, of me using magic in my knitting. They were old-fashioned like that and very rigid. They believed I should learn the craft. Since I so enjoyed their company at the vampire knitting club meetings, I was trying very hard to improve. And I was getting better. I could knit and purl, and if I paid attention, I could even do them in the correct order. I still had a terrible time when I dropped stitches. And whenever anyone mentioned the soothing benefits of knitting, I wanted to strangle them. However, it was undeniable that I was improving. As someone who owned a knitting shop, that was a very good thing.

An older woman came over to watch Clara unpicking my work and spoke to me. "Do you really own a knitting shop?"

"Yes. Cardinal Woolsey's, in Oxford."

Sylvia said, "It's the most marvelous shop. Lucy stocks nothing but the highest quality of knitting and crochet supplies as well as patterns and notions. And her classes are excellent."

It was great that she was doing such a good sales job on my shop, but I wondered why. The last thing I needed was a bunch of witch hunters coming to Cardinal Woolsey's. The only thing worse would be vampire hunters.

But when she looked at me and gave me the ghost of a wink, I waited, knowing she had something in mind. She said, "In fact, she's expanding her classes." *Expanding my classes?* I had trouble finding teachers for the few I did offer.

I gazed at her in astonishment as she continued, "In fact, if there's enough interest, perhaps we could offer one here in Moreton-Under-Wychwood."

Who was this "we" she referred to?

Before I could speak, the woman who'd been watching Clara broke into a delighted smile. "Oh, that would be wonderful. Why, there are at least half a dozen of us here who love to knit. I know people say you can order things online, but I don't like the computer. I like to see and touch before I buy."

I might be a novice witch who'd narrowly escaped being attacked by a mob, but I was also a businesswoman, and I took pride, as did my undead grandmother, in growing our little business. I looked at Sylvia. "If you'd be available to teach the classes here, I could bring a selection of wools and patterns. In fact," I said, warming to the idea, "If anyone finds something online and they're unsure, email us, and I can bring merchandise out for you to look at. No need to buy in advance."

I had never seen anything so astonishing in my life as the way the atmosphere in that café changed as the villagers went from a bunch of suspicious witch-haters to retirees and stay-at-home moms excited about knitting classes.

"Certainly. I've been developing some Fair Isle patterns. I could teach a simple one for the novices and something more complex for the more experienced knitter. What do you think, Lucy?"

I'm sure my smile looked like that of someone who's heard the punchline to a joke and they don't get it. Fair Isle? Wasn't that a place in Scotland?

All the knitters seemed super excited about this, but I was still silent. Clara leaned closer and whispered, "Fair Isle is when you knit with two colors at the same time to make a pattern." There's a reason why Clara is one of my favorite vampires.

"Sure," I said. "What a great idea."

The woman had been so excited, but now she grew solemn. "But where will we hold a class? Normally, I'd suggest the village hall, but the police have cordoned it off."

There was a moment of awful silence as we all were jerked back to the reality of yesterday's death.

"Joanna? What about your farmhouse?" I recognized the speaker. She was the lady who'd run the white elephant yesterday. She seemed like a sensible woman and as eager as I to bring goodwill to the café.

Joanna turned out to be a tall, stylish woman who looked more London than Moreton-Under-Wychwood. "What a wonderful idea. I'd be delighted to hold the lessons at our farm. We run the old farmhouse as a holiday let and corporate retreat." She said it would hold thirty people, and the way interest was already brewing, I suspected we might have that many. Never one to let business slip away, I pulled out my phone and immediately started a list, adding people's emails.

A few who signed up said they had friends who would be interested and began texting them immediately, worried the class would fill up before they had a chance to register.

The woman whose two online dates had both canceled on her suddenly said, "But how do we know that she isn't a witch?"

No wonder she had trouble getting a date with those interpersonal skills. Fortunately, before I could say anything, the lady who had offered her farmhouse laughed. "Really, Sarah, what kind of witch would run a knitting shop?"

Sarah looked unconvinced for a moment, and then as everyone seemed to be in agreement with the woman who owned the farmhouse, she backed down. "No, I suppose not."

Dodged that bullet.

And speaking of dodging bullets, or not dodging arrows, what I particularly loved about Sylvia's strategy was the way it gave me a perfectly good reason to return to Moreton-Under-Wychwood. Perhaps I didn't have a strong reason to get involved in trying to help solve this murder, but I was fond of my cousin Violet, and I didn't like that her neighbors were looking askance at her.

Margaret Twig seemed as though she could take care of herself. However, since she was the head of my coven, I supposed I should show a little respect and try to help her if I could.

There was so much enthusiasm about knitting classes that Sylvia said she'd be happy to start the classes one evening this week. "Lucy?"

"So long as we have at least ten confirmed students by

tonight, then yes. We can start Wednesday." I knew from experience that until a student had booked and paid, there was no certainty that they'd show up. We agreed that Sylvia would provide the patterns and both beginner and advanced would use the same wools to make the logistics easier.

We settled on Wednesday evening for the first class. Joanna, the woman who owned the farmhouse, said I was welcome to come and see her space. I wasn't only thinking about how suitable it was for classes. I sensed she was well-known and well-liked in this community. She might have some insights into the personalities involved.

I was about to suggest to Sylvia that we should head out when a man entered the café. All conversation suddenly hushed. The silence was even more strained than when the witches had walked in. He looked to be in his early fifties, ruggedly good looking, or had been. He looked like a man who was normally quite pleased with his life, but his eyes were currently strained and red-rimmed. Nora, the dead woman's best friend, rose from her chair and walked forward with her arms out. "Oh, Jason. I'm so sorry. Come and sit down."

I didn't need any magical powers to figure out that this was the husband of the dead woman. Perhaps Sylvia and I wouldn't leave the café quite yet. Since Clara had left her cappuccino untouched, I began to sip it. I watched as the new widower settled himself beside his dead wife's friend and her husband.

They put their heads close together and began to talk in soft voices.

"Such a tragedy," the woman who liked to knit said. "The four of them did everything together. Now it's only three. And Jason looks so sad, poor love. Perhaps I'll bake him a pie."

A woman at the next table heard her and agreed that would be a nice gesture. From the enthusiasm of the local women deciding what type of food they would take the new widower, I did not think Jason Palmer was going to starve anytime soon.

Still, these neighbors demonstrated such community kind-ness that I could hardly reconcile so much generosity with the sharp suspicion they had showed the witches earlier. I had to remember that as nice as these people might be on the surface, there was a dark side to this village. Somewhere here was a murderer.

CHAPTER 9

*J*oanna Newman, the owner of the farmhouse, lived about two miles from the center of town. She said there was a shortcut, a pleasant walk across the fields, and I would normally have been tempted. However, Clara and Sylvia wouldn't want to tramp across fields on a sunny spring day, so I said our time was a little tight and that we would drive to her home.

Also, I wanted a few minutes alone with Sylvia to plan our strategy. I took Joanna's address and told her we'd meet her at her home in thirty minutes.

We drove down a narrow country road following Joanna's directions and came to a brightly painted sign that said Nickleby Farm. Below the sign were hanging baskets overflowing with spring flowers.

We drove down quite a long drive. There were two horses in the field who stopped chewing grass and looked up at us, presumably hoping we would stop and bring something like carrots or apples. However, when we continued driving, they put their heads back down to the green lawn.

Any idea I'd had that the farmhouse would be old and

shabby were soon put to rout. The farmhouse was a beautiful old stone building with dormer windows and an orchard behind. On the other side of the orchard, a swimming pool glinted, and beside that was a tennis court and then something that might be mini-golf.

When we pulled up, Joanna opened the green painted door and greeted us. She let us into a large room that was part high-end farmhouse kitchen and part sitting room. "We rent the farmhouse, you see, for corporate retreats, big family gatherings and weddings. So there's plenty of room downstairs."

She toured us around briskly as though we might be thinking about a corporate retreat. She pointed out the excellent lighting, a good number of plugs for laptops, how well the kitchen was stocked and that there were six bedrooms upstairs. "There's a full bathroom and a powder room down that hall and two more bathrooms upstairs."

I thought it seemed perfect and I said so. "If you're kind enough to offer the farmhouse for lessons, then naturally your class will be free."

She didn't look as though she needed the money, but still she looked quite pleased at my offer. "That's very kind of you. Thank you. I'll probably bring my daughter, as well, but I'm most happy to pay for her."

I really wanted to get Joanna gossiping, and so I said, "I hope we get enough people. It would be so much fun to run a class here. Do you know many people in the area?"

"Oh, my dear, yes. Bill's parents owned this farm, you see. We used to come up from London on weekends and bring the children. We spent most of our summers here. The property came to Bill when his parents died and we built the corporate retreat and, when we retired, moved up here permanently. Because Bill grew up here, we've never been looked on as outsiders. So, yes, I think it's safe to say I know most of the people around here," she twinkled at me, "and most of the gossip."

I laughed as though gossip were the last thing on my mind. "But what a terrible shock for the whole community to lose that lovely woman yesterday."

She immediately sobered. "It's unthinkable. Elizabeth Palmer really was a lovely woman. Everyone liked her. It's such a terrible accident."

She drifted to one of the overstuffed couches and sat down, and with a slight nod of my head indicating the vampires should follow me, I sat down across from her. Clara and Sylvia sat slightly back in armchairs. I had to admit, this would be a very comfortable space in which to knit. For those, unlike me, who found knitting a comfortable occupation.

I nodded. "Of course I only met her briefly, but she was so excited about her twenty-fifth anniversary. She said she and her husband were going on a cruise."

"Yes. She talked of little else. Things weren't always easy for Elizabeth and Jason. Frankly, he wasn't the businessman that her father was. I think money was sometimes a bit tight. Still, they were pulling out all the stops for their anniversary trip. I suppose Jason will cancel it now. I wonder if Tony and Nora will go in any case. It seems a shame not to now that it's all booked and presumably paid for."

"Tony and Nora?"

"Oh yes, the four of them were great friends. They were all going on the cruise together."

Had I heard a certain something in her tone? Or was my busy brain searching for possible murder motives? I didn't know, but I found myself asking whether the four of them had always been close. What I really meant was how close.

Like me, Joanna seemed to hear the meaning beneath the words. She said, "Nora and Jason are both keen golfers. Neither

Elizabeth nor Tony cared for the sport, so Nora and Jason went off golfing together quite often."

Her tone seemed a tad too breezy. Sometimes talking in subtext was too tiring. I decided to be very American and ask a direct question. "Did you ever think it was more than golf between them?"

If she was taken aback by my directness, she didn't show it. "There were rumors, of course. But you know how people can be. Tony and Liz didn't seem to mind, and if they were happy to see their spouses go off and play golf, then what business was it of anyone else?"

"But now Elizabeth's dead," I reminded her. "If it was murder, the police will be looking for motives."

Her head jerked up and her eyes widened, startled, as though she hadn't connected Elizabeth's death with the possibility of her husband having an affair. "What are you suggesting? That Jason killed his wife? Or that Nora killed her best friend? It's unthinkable. Besides, they were both at the fair. Everyone was at the fair."

Certainly, Nora had been in the tent with Violet at the time of the murder. But didn't that provide her with an excellent alibi? She could plan the murder in cahoots with her lover, Elizabeth's husband. She could've made sure that her friend was headed down the path toward the archery field and somehow let him know.

I hadn't seen her go into the tent. I'd been too busy trying to catch up with Elizabeth. Nora could easily have sent off a quick text before her psychic reading.

I thanked Joanna and got to my feet before I came across as a prying busybody. But one thing was still bothering me. "Did Tony and Nora seem completely happy to you?" I had seen them briefly in the coffee shop this morning, and there had been no sign of discord, not even when Jason joined them.

She said, "Tony would do absolutely anything for his wife. He worships her."

"I can see that everyone is on edge. It must be awful having one of your neighbors murdered in a lovely, quiet village like this one."

Joanna looked at me oddly. "I think people are particularly worried because it's not the first murder we've ever had here."

My eyes widened in shock. "This isn't the first one?" I really, really hoped the first one had nothing to do with witches being victims.

She turned to look outside, as though the story were written on the windowpane. "It happened, oh, it must be thirty years ago now. A man named Grayson Timmins surprised someone in the act of robbing him and was bludgeoned to death."

"How awful." The retired detective had mentioned the case to me only yesterday, and in all the drama, I'd actually forgotten.

No wonder those people were freaking out. "You think there could be a connection between Elizabeth's death and a cold case?"

She turned her head back toward me, and her eyes looked both sad and a little frightened. "One has to wonder."

"Is there any link between them?" Once more I was certain I could read her thoughts. "Or could it be the work of a deranged serial killer?"

Her eyes fluttered shut. "I've got the grandchildren coming this weekend, Lucy. Please don't say those words."

Sylvia spoke, "I think, if I were you, I would reschedule your grandchildren."

CHAPTER 10

I thanked Joanna again for offering the space for the lessons.

She rose and handed me a brochure. "It's got all my contact information and directions to get here. Don't you worry. I can almost guarantee we'll have thirty people at your knitting class. Certainly getting to your ten won't be a problem."

The two vampires and I said goodbye, and I pulled on my sunglasses while Clara and Sylvia put on their big sun hats and gathered their parasols. Then we piled into the little Ford once more and headed back to Oxford.

I complimented Sylvia on her excellent maneuver suggesting the lessons and Clara in saving the day by coming in looking for knitting help. They both laughed and Clara said, "I'd love to take credit, but it was Rafe's idea."

The gears ground as I changed from second to third, not clutching properly. Of course it was Rafe's idea.

As we drove back to Oxford, the three of us discussed what we'd learned. "I know you were both watching Joanna. Did you get the idea that the relationship between Nora and Elizabeth's husband, Jason, wasn't completely platonic?"

Neither of them rushed into speech. Clara, who always thought the best of people, said, "It could be a warm friendship between people who have known each other a very long while. If their spouses didn't mind and they both were golf fanatics, then perhaps there's nothing more sinister than unkind village gossip."

Sylvia was both more cynical and more worldly-wise. She was sitting behind me. I looked in the rearview mirror to try and catch her expression, but all I saw was the back seat. It was hard to remember sometimes that these women who'd become my friends were vampires and didn't have reflections. I used my words. "Sylvia? What do you think?"

"Joanna didn't seem to be the kind of person who gossips for gossip's sake. You know the old saying, 'Where there's smoke, there's fire'?"

"But there's also the possibility of a serial killer," I reminded her. "What if the same person who killed Grayson Timmins also killed Elizabeth?"

"Thirty years is a long time between attacks. I would say that looking into the relationship between the husband of the dead woman—Jason, was it?—and her friend Nora would be more worth exploring."

"But how? We're not the police."

"Let's get dear Nora to sign up for the knitting classes. Yes," she said, ruminating on the idea. "That's what we must do."

"Please don't ask me to make a spell that will encourage her to come to the class. I don't think I'm up to it."

"I'll use my own talents."

"Vampire talents?"

"Mostly charm and persuasion, and I was born with those."

I needed to remember that Sylvia resented any implication that she might be more powerful now than when she'd been alive, since she'd so clearly been spectacular. A famous stage and screen actress of the 1920s, she found it cruelly difficult now to be a person who had to fade into the background, who needed someone else to apply her makeup and who could never see her own face in the mirror.

"How will you encourage Nora to join the knitting class?" I wasn't sure I'd be interested in going to a crafting class if my best friend had just been killed.

"I'm not sure yet. We'll get Theodore to help us. He can make some posters. Clara and I can go back to the village tomorrow and put them up in a few strategic places. Naturally, the class is going to fill up without any need for extra advertising, but we'll find out where Nora lives and works and make sure she gets a poster."

"Well, good luck." We were passing through Woodstock, and traffic was Sunday-afternoon busy.

Her voice was laced with laughter when she answered. "Lucy, you're coming with us, of course. You have to drive."

"Sylvia, you have a perfectly good car of your own and a driver." I shifted gears, never an easy task with my left hand. I wasn't sure I'd ever get used to this driving on the wrong side of the road business, and the last thing I needed was another precarious trip out to Moreton-Under-Wychwood. "Besides, tomorrow is Monday. My shop will be open."

"I cannot drive into that small village in my chauffeured Bentley. They'll think I'm showing off."

Showing off had never seemed to bother Sylvia before.

"And besides, the sooner we get this murder business solved, the better it will be for you and your fellow witches."

I wasn't sure how much help I could be, since my sleuthing abilities were amateur at best. Still, she was right about the Bentley.

∾

68

I LET the vampires out in the back lane, and then I wedged the tiny Ford in the equally tiny parking spot behind my shop and flat. We went into the back door off the garden that led up the stairs and into my flat.

The mouthwatering smell of gingersnaps assailed my nostrils, and I immediately felt better. I turned to the others. "Gran's upstairs. Why don't you come up?"

Clara yawned. "I'm rather tired, but perhaps I'll come for a short visit before I go to bed."

Sylvia was like Rafe and seemed to survive on catnaps, never appearing tired. The three of us went upstairs. Sure enough, Gran was bustling about in the kitchen. She pulled me into a hug as soon as she saw me. "I heard what happened." She looked worried. "Mabel and I came back from Dublin as soon as we heard. Lucy, you must be careful. Of course witches and pagans are much more tolerated these days, but fear still makes normal people do terrible things." I recalled the behavior of the villagers in the coffee shop this morning and shuddered. I had firsthand experience of what she was talking about, and I really could've done without it.

"I'm more worried about Violet. I'm fairly protected here in Oxford, but she and Aunt Lavinia both live in the village." I struggled with myself and then said, "Margaret Twig lives near there, too. I really felt animosity toward them."

"It's the murder," Sylvia said. "It's got everyone in that village edgy."

I felt much less edgy immediately. Homemade cookies somehow kept grimness at bay. "Gran, I can't believe you made gingersnaps. You must be tired from traveling."

"Not at all. It was a lovely, restful weekend. I was tempted to make something different. But today I thought you needed something familiar and well-loved."

Like my Gran. "I do. Never stop making them. They remind me of being here with you when I was younger." They made me feel safe. In a world that had become increasingly chaotic, I craved anything that would give me the illusion of safety.

We immediately began telling Gran about our day.

I became aware of him before he appeared at the top of the stairs from the direction of my shop, and not because he knocked, rang the bell, or in any other way acted like a normal visitor. Rafe strolled in. "I smelled baking," he said, as though that excused his behavior. He nodded to the three vampires and then came and put his hands on my shoulders and studied my face. "How are you holding up?"

"I'm all right." It was a lie, and he knew it.

"There's something very odd about that woman's death," he said as though he were discussing one of his rare manuscripts and he'd discovered an oddity. I couldn't help it, I giggled. "Really? You think so? A woman in the middle of a fair is struck down by a longbow and you think there's something slightly peculiar going on?"

He ignored my sarcasm. "Not a longbow, actually."

Honestly, it was an exercise in self-restraint not to roll my eyes constantly when he was around. The man was so annoying because he knew everything, not only because he'd been around for hundreds of years, but because he was naturally intelligent. Super intelligent, in fact. "What kind of bow was it, Rafe?" Okay, I asked it in a snarky kid with attitude in the back of the classroom kind of way. But, again, he ignored my sarcasm. "I'm not sure. But I suspect it was a recurve. It's smaller than a longbow, the arrow travels faster, and the aim is more accurate."

"Okay, I'm not exactly up on medieval archery techniques. Longbow, shortbow, recurve, whatever. An arrow killed her."

He shook his head. "Lucy, in a case like this, I suspect that detail is everything."

"A case? What are we? Holmes and Watson?" Actually, it wasn't a bad comparison. Rafe was the insomniac with the brilliant mind and an eye for detail. He also had a socially unacceptable appetite. I, on the other hand, was partly comic relief and the one who got to ask him the dumb questions, which he could then answer, showing off his brilliance. It was very annoying.

At least I didn't write up the cases in order to give a man with an oversize ego an even fatter head.

He said, "I think it would be a very good idea to make a visit to the Wychwood Bowmen."

I shuddered. "Do you really think they're interested in talking to us?"

"I think they could be persuaded."

He never said things like that if he didn't mean them. "What did you have in mind?"

"Tomorrow, they have an afternoon drop-in session for members and potential members. It's a good way to get to know the club and ask some questions."

"And you know this how?"

He looked at me like I was being a bit dense. "I looked it up on the Internet."

I don't know why I'd assumed he'd consulted the vampire network. Sometimes, everyday tools worked just as well.

I accepted a cookie and the fresh cup of coffee that Gran had brewed me. And I began to pace. I trusted everyone in the room right now, and we'd already been through some difficult times together. In the theory that five brains are better than one, especially if one of them is at genius level, I asked aloud, "Who kills a woman in the middle of a fair?"

I took a sip of coffee and put my mug down on the coffee table. "And was the death an accident? Or was it murder? And if it was murder, was Elizabeth Palmer the intended victim? Or is this somehow random?"

"Good questions," Sylvia said.

I continued, "And who kills someone with an arrow? It's so, I don't know, historic."

Rafe nodded. "I've been thinking that, too. If it was indeed murder, and I suspect it was, then was the mode of death a message in itself?"

I stared at him. "You mean like using a bow and arrow was itself a message? But the person receiving it would end up dead."

"Unless it was a warning to someone else?"

I hadn't thought of that.

He began to pace now, too. It was annoying that we both had that habit when we were thinking. "They don't do it so much anymore, at least not in England, but public punishment and executions were commonplace. People would come from miles around and bring the children to see a highwayman hung or a disfavored queen have her head chopped off." He looked up. "Putting a thief in the stocks in the middle of the village square was a good deterrent to other thieves."

If I was following his reasoning, what he was trying to say was... I didn't know what he was trying to say.

I wasn't sure he knew, either. I thought he was puzzling out something as he was saying the words. "What if Elizabeth Palmer was involved in something she shouldn't have been? And she had a partner or partners? By killing her in that public way, the murderer sent her associates a very clear message."

"You mean the way someone once tried to kill me to stop me from snooping?"

He smiled rather grimly. "Exactly like that."

It did put a whole new complexion on this mystery. But everywhere you looked at it, the thing was a mystery. "We don't know enough. We don't know enough about Elizabeth, about her background. We don't know enough about her husband or friends. And, apparently, this isn't the first murder they've had in Moreton-Under-Wychwood."

He glanced at me oddly. "No doubt they've had dozens of murders over the centuries. This is a very old village. But no doubt you're referring to the unsolved murder from thirty years ago."

Whatever muscle controlled the eye roll was really getting a workout today. "Yes, Professor Smarty-Pants, I was referring to the cold case of thirty years ago. What do you know about it?"

"Not much. I wasn't living in the area at the time."

I related what Joanna had told us about the murder, then looked around. "What do you think? Could these two deaths be connected in some way?"

Sylvia spoke up. "I would think it's impossible to know the answer to that until we solve both murders."

I let out a sound that was half grunt, half wail. "Solve two murders?" It was all right for them. They were permanently retired and rich. I had a shop to run. "Look, I wish you well in your sleuthing, but I have to think of Cardinal Woolsey's. Besides, I've got to get everything ready for this new class we're now running on Wednesday." Which reminded me, I needed to run down and get it all set up on the computer.

I wasn't going to drive all the way to Moreton-Under-Wych-wood with my supplies and Sylvia ready to teach a lesson without being sure I had enough students. Never mind about solving murders, I also had a business to run.

"Lucy, you're coming with us to Moreton-Under-Wychwood tomorrow," Sylvia reminded me.

"What about Cardinal Woolsey's?"

Gran was the one I most thought would be on my side, since she had started the shop. She said, "Violet could run it. Violet's perfectly competent when she puts her mind to it. Besides, you're doing this for her."

And then Rafe said, "You're also coming with me to visit the Wychwood Bowmen tomorrow afternoon. I very much doubt whether you'll make it into the shop at all tomorrow."

Well, now that my entire day was spoken for, I could pretty much throw out my agenda book. If I had one.

I threw up my hands in frustration. "Fine!" In truth, I might've argued with them, except I was delighted at the prospect of a day out. I didn't really want them doing all the sleuthing without me. It was a lot more fun to uncover clues in bright spring sunshine than to be stuck inside with wool all day. Naturally, I wouldn't say that to Violet when she showed up to work tomorrow.

Rafe said, "There are too many things we don't know."

I looked at him. "Do the police have the cause of death yet?" He had connections everywhere, and we often had the coroner's report before the actual detectives did.

He said, "The heart was pierced through. Death would have been practically instantaneous. I believe they've interviewed most of the fairgoers and haven't gathered anything terribly useful."

"No one saw a Robin Hood type headed for the village hall?"

"Sadly, no."

"But it was the arrow that killed her."

"No question. And, if it was aimed at Elizabeth Palmer, it was an excellent shot. We're looking at an expert bowman."

"Or woman," Sylvia said, tossing her head back. "I played Joan of Arc in a film once. I studied archery for the part. I have to say, I was quite good." She smiled. "At archery, I mean. As an actress, I was superb."

Instinctively, I turned to Rafe, who nodded. "Yes. Good point, Sylvia. A reasonably strong woman could have made that shot."

I looked at Gran and thought about inheritances. I'd been an underemployed cubicle worker when Gran had changed my life forever. She'd never told me that when she passed away I would become the new owner of both Cardinal Woolsey's knitting shop and the flat above it.

Of course, I could've sold the property, but every day I was glad that I hadn't. This life suited me, and I never would have discovered that if Gran hadn't made me her beneficiary. People's lives changed every day because of wills, life insurance policies and inheritances of one kind or another. "Who benefits from Elizabeth's death? Is there a life insurance policy? Did she have a will?"

Rafe nodded at me approvingly. "Good. You're thinking strategically. I've asked Theodore to have a snoop around and see if he can find the answer to those questions." So, as usual, Rafe was way ahead of me. Still, I'd found my way there in the end.

Theodore had been a policeman in life. Now he kept busy as a part-time private investigator, but he also took great pleasure in painting scenes for amateur theater productions and, of course, knitting. In fact, between all the members of the vampire knitting club, we had a lot of talent, a lot of experience and, perhaps most important, any number of creatures with nothing but time on their hands and the ability to slide through the streets at night, where they could unobtrusively listen in on conversations and see things that they perhaps weren't intended to see.

The vampires tended to have super senses, so they could see better than humans, definitely hear better and smell better. They were like hunting dogs with human brains and communication abilities.

We didn't normally meet on Sunday nights, but I never had any trouble getting my vampires together for an impromptu knitting session. I suggested we meet that very night in the back room of my shop. The more quickly we got the vampires helping with this case, the faster Elizabeth Palmer would receive justice.

There was a trapdoor from the back room of my shop that led down to the tunnels underneath Oxford where most of the vampires lived. Clara stood up. "Excellent idea, Lucy. I'll let everyone know. And now, if you don't mind, I'm going to head to bed." Gran had been surreptitiously yawning, too. I wondered if more recent vampires needed more sleep than the older ones, but I had no idea, and it felt like an awkward question to ask. Sylvia said she'd go down with them.

Rafe lingered behind. He fiddled with things and put them down. Behavior that was very unlike him. Then suddenly, he turned to me. "Do we need to talk?"

What had we just been doing? Salsa lessons? "Talk about what?"

He fussed some more. He picked up one of Gran's Victorian china dolls that I didn't have the heart to move from an upper shelf where they'd been ever since I could remember. He straightened her lace cap and replaced her on the shelf. In an awkward tone, he said, "About us?"

I burst out laughing. "Rafe, you must be the first vampire in all of history to utter the 'We have to talk' line."

He straightened the next doll on the shelf. "I feel awkward, that's all."

He'd kissed me back in February in a magical wood on a silvery moonlit night. We'd both agreed at the time that it would be a moment that existed out of time and out of history. Something that we wouldn't refer to again. Had I thought about that kiss since it happened? Of course I had. I'm female, human, and it was a great kiss. But I did not want to have the talk.

I had no idea where this odd relationship with Rafe was going. At times, I imagined being with him forever. But the trouble was my definition of forever was the lifespan of a normal mortal. His forever was, well, forever.

I would age, and he wouldn't. I would die; he wouldn't. As

much as I cared for him, I had no interest in becoming a vampire myself. I had enough trouble imagining what I'd do next weekend, never mind the next millennium. So, for now, I was content to let that kiss remain in the magical world, at least until I was ready to make some decisions.

He finally stopped fiddling and turned to face me. His face was serious, and the way he was looking at me made my heart speed up. "I care for you," he said simply.

Why is it that the simplest lines can mean more than a hundred bouquets or long, flowery speeches?

Maybe because I knew how deeply Rafe meant those words.

I was tempted to tell him that I cared for him, too. But then he'd kiss me again. And my life would become more complicated than I was able to handle.

"I know," I replied.

CHAPTER 11

The vampire knitting club met that night, at our usual time of ten p.m. Those who lived under my shop came up, some of them yawning, having just woken up, some looking ready for the night's adventures.

I was at the end of my day and tired, but they all looked as fresh as a bunch of bloodsucking daisies. My heart sank just a little when I saw that Silence Buggins was among them. Silence had been on a trip to visit another Victorian-era vampire she'd known in life. It had been so peaceful without her. If ever anyone was badly named, it was Silence. Her name had come from one of the virtues as was common in Victorian times, but sadly, it was not a virtue that poor Silence possessed.

She was the biggest chatterbox I'd ever known. Also a braggart, and that was an unfortunate combination. She was usually convinced she was right. To give her credit, sometimes she was. She was definitely convinced that modern society was full of moral decay. She had brought not only her Victorian values with her but her Victorian garb. She still wore button-up leather boots. She wore high-necked dresses with lace collars and, though I had never pried, I was convinced she wore corsets. Her hair was always piled high on her head, and she never left the house without her hat on. In many other cities in the world she would've looked like an oddity, but fortunately, Oxford was full of oddities.

Theodore didn't come out of the trapdoor with the rest of them—he walked in the front door of my shop with Rafe a little before ten. I could tell at once that he had news. He looked altogether too pleased with himself, and his innocent baby blue eyes were sparkling. No doubt he'd already told Rafe everything. I was becoming accustomed to Rafe always knowing everything before I did. Well, not everything. I still managed to surprise him from time to time.

Everyone settled down with their knitting projects. I was experimenting with a pattern for a blanket that was entirely made of knitted squares. I was really quite pleased with myself, as this allowed me to work on one square until I ruined it or got bored. The idea was that you learned your stitches for each square and it ended up like a knitted sampler. I was pretty much sticking to stocking stitch in various colors, though. I didn't want to run before I could walk.

Sylvia was trying to convince me to try her Fair Isle project for the knitting class at Moreton-Under-Wychwood, but even looking at the pattern she'd drawn on a grid made my head hurt. The beginner project was a square with a geometric pattern running across the middle in a stripe. It looked like a line of stylized tulips. She said the beginner one could be backed and turned into a pot holder, or she was creating a sweater for the more advanced knitters.

Anyway, I pulled out my square of stocking stitch. I looked at it dispassionately, flattening the square out on my lap. I loved the purple color, but I could see that my tension hadn't been even, and there were a couple of suspicious-looking holes where I'd dropped stitches and hadn't noticed, but overall, for a project of mine, it wasn't too bad.

Since the vampires were used to my usual disasters, I was rewarded with extravagant praise, far more than my piddling effort deserved. Still, I was not immune to flattery, and I drank it in the way a wilting plant drinks in water.

Hester, the eternally sulky teenager, had also returned. She'd been visiting friends in LA, and I'd hoped she might decide to stay there.

"How was your trip?" Clara asked her politely.

She heaved a tragic sigh as though the entire trip had been a huge imposition. "Dreadful. That place is sunny all the time. I could barely leave the house. And the nightlife that everyone gets so excited about was rubbish."

"You got carded, didn't you?" Theodore asked. "I told you that fake ID wasn't going to work."

She glared at him. "Anyway, I had an awful time." She picked up her knitting, a black shawl of some sort, and scowled at it.

Gran was working on a sleeveless lace top for me, something I could wear in the summertime when I was working in the shop. It was a lovely shade of mauve, which I had chosen myself. She asked me to stand up so that she could get the length right. I had argued that she should make something for herself this time. Honestly, the vampires were always making me things. My closets were jammed with the most gorgeous knitted goods, and I was having trouble finding new places to put them all. However, Gran insisted that she had several lifetimes of knitted sweaters already. And since I'd seen so many of them in the flat, I knew this was true.

I made myself feel better by knowing that there were going to be some very nice finds in the charity shops very soon.

Dr. Christopher Bartlett was working on an incredibly complex waistcoat. He liked to wear snazzy waistcoats. Sylvia was crocheting herself a new bedspread, all in black and silver lace. It was going to be beautiful.

Theodore pulled out a pair of socks to work on, but I could tell he wasn't in the mood. He still had his private investigator's persona on, and he couldn't quite make the shift to a knitter. Not that I wanted him to, not until he'd shared his findings.

I waited until both Silence and Hester had said as much as they wanted to about their trips. Well, Silence would've gone on talking about the delights of Edinburgh longer than she'd actually been away if Sylvia hadn't gently stopped the flow of words by telling her there'd been a murder in Moreton-Under-Wychwood.

Hester dropped the shawl she was halfheartedly knitting into her lap, and her mouth fell open in disgust. "I can't believe it. I always miss everything interesting around here. What happened? Who was it? Anyone we know?"

Gran gently reminded her that someone had died.

Hester rolled her eyes. "Big deal. I died."

"Theodore," I said in a bright tone. "Tell us what you discovered."

Theodore's pale face seemed to grow rounder, as it did when he was pleased. "Thank you for asking, Lucy. I have to say, I've been quite productive. You wanted to know who gained in Elizabeth Palmer's death." Modestly, he cast down his eyes and said, "I was able to get a peek at the will."

No doubt it was better not to pry into his methods.

"Everything goes to her husband."

My eyebrows rose. "And by everything?"

"They co-owned the house, the business, and she had a few stocks and bonds that her father had left her." I could tell there was more, and so I waited. He settled back, his socks completely forgotten in his lap. Most everyone else knitted on while still listening, except me and Rafe.

Theodore continued, "It's a curious thing. The car dealership that she inherited from her father—well, I suppose they both inherited it, since she was married by then and Jason runs the business—it's not doing well at all."

"Really?"

He shook his head. "I took a quick look at the books. I would say that business is teetering on bankruptcy."

Sylvia glanced up from her lacework. "A car dealership in a small town like that has probably always been precarious."

He nodded at her. "I thought the same thing, so I checked back. When they inherited that business, it was quite successful. Flush with cash and almost no debt." He shook his head. "There's almost nothing now but debt."

"So the husband's run the business into the ground?"

Theodore nodded sadly. "He's also mortgaged the house. Essentially, that couple was on the brink of financial ruin."

"Did Elizabeth know?" I thought back to that sunny woman I'd spoken to only yesterday at the fair. She was looking forward to the twenty-fifth anniversary cruise. She'd bought that beautiful silver watch for her husband. She had not looked like a woman in dire financial straits. She'd looked comfortable, prosperous.

I shook my head, answering my own question. "I'm almost certain she didn't know."

Theodore said, "I think you may be right. Naturally, since both the business and the home were in both their names, she signed both documents, but I'm not certain it's actually her signature."

"You mean he forged her signature?"

He shrugged. "Easy enough to do. Husbands and wives sign for each other frequently, and I doubt the bank would've looked particularly closely."

I'd seen Jason, and he'd looked genuinely sad. I didn't think you could fake that kind of grief. "I can't believe Jason would kill his wife for half of a failing business and mortgaged home."

Sylvia said, "No. But he might if it would stop her finding

out. They were wealthy when they married, and in twenty-five years, he's managed to throw away everything. Not only their lifetime of work, but that of her parents."

I could see that Elizabeth would be angry, and Jason had definitely screwed up, but was it enough to kill for? Theodore continued, "Of course, as is very common in jointly owned businesses, there was a life insurance policy."

"Of course," Sylvia said quite softly. Her hands moved with lightning speed creating the lace. It was like watching a starry night, the black and then the sparkle of silver.

Rafe said, "Tell us more."

"The will was quite standard, really. In the event of either of their deaths, the business went entirely to the other person. It was the same with other personal goods. However, they also had a million pound life insurance policy."

Hester blinked. "Blimey, a million pounds. I'd kill somebody if I could get a million pounds out of it."

"Hester," Clara said reprovingly. "That's not funny. You will be rich soon enough. Just bide your time and follow our advice."

She kicked her foot forward. "But that's so boring. It takes ages and ages. I want lots of money now."

What a cruel twist of fate that poor Hester had been turned into a vampire during those difficult teenage years. Imagine being a miserable teenager for all eternity. I looked at the rest of the vampires. No doubt they weren't thrilled about living with a cranky adolescent for all eternity, either. It was a double curse.

To smooth over an awkward moment, I said, "Hester's right. A million pounds is a lot of money."

However, I didn't want to think Jason had killed his wife, not without a lot more proof. "Elizabeth seemed happy in her marriage. I don't think we should jump to conclusions."

Rafe said, "Lucy's right. The impoverished husband is the obvious suspect, but not the only one."

Theodore shrugged. "I was a policeman for many years. In my experience, it's usually the most obvious suspects who turn out to be guilty." He looked around the room at all the busily knitting vampires and then back at me. "Besides, there's more."

I had thought there might be. "Would that be anything to do with Nora Betts? The woman who was Elizabeth Palmer's best friend? Who went on golfing trips with Jason Palmer?"

He nodded as though I were an apt pupil. "Well done, Lucy. Yes indeed. I haven't had time yet to visit some of the places where Nora and Jason stayed together. My telephone inquiries have confirmed that they always rented separate rooms on their golfing trips. However, the resorts they stayed in, although they had golfing, weren't always the best areas for golf. I would've said the hotels they chose were more suited to romance."

"Oh, poor Elizabeth."

"I'm going to take a little road trip and visit a few of them. Someone, somewhere, has seen or heard something. And if they have, I'll find out." Theodore's innocent eyes sparkled. "People tell me things."

The room went quiet with all of us busily knitting. How could Elizabeth have been so excited about her twenty-fifth anniversary trip if she'd known her husband was having an affair? Why, she'd bought him that lovely gift. Would she have done that if he was betraying her with her best friend?

I looked up and gasped. "The watch," I said aloud.

Rafe's gaze immediately went to mine. "Watch?"

"What happened to it?" I shook my head in puzzlement, then realized no one had a clue what I was talking about. "Elizabeth showed me a watch that she bought for her husband right before she had her fortune told. After Violet's disastrous fortune, she was quite upset, and I followed her, trying to catch up to her and put a forgetting spell on her. Before I reached her, she was killed. What happened to the watch?"

His eyes narrowed on my face. "Could she have put it into her handbag? Or perhaps a pocket?"

"It was such a warm day. She wasn't wearing a coat or a jacket." Had she carried a handbag? I concentrated hard and brought it into focus. A straw summer bag. There had definitely been room to put a watch into it. Still, I would quite like to know if they had recovered that watch. If Ian had been the detective in charge, I'd have phoned him. But DI Thomas didn't know me. He definitely wouldn't share confidential information.

Rafe said, "I have contacts in the police. I'll ask whether a watch was found among her things."

"Thanks."

He asked me what kind of watch it was, and I tried to describe it to him. "It was a man's pocket watch. I know it was sterling, because Elizabeth Palmer showed me the hallmarks. There were four of them. I recognized the British lion, of course. There was an anchor, which Elizabeth said meant it had been made near Birmingham. There was a mark for the date. A 'D,' I think. And initials. The watch also had a curious vine pattern on the front of it. I'm sure I'd recognize it again if I saw it."

In an acidic voice, Sylvia said, "We don't go in for silver much around here."

I was mortified. I supposed it was as bad a blunder as asking her how she liked her reflection in the mirror.

Rafe said, "I have a book of sterling silver marks. If you recognize the initials, we can find out who made it. And the 'D' should tell us when."

I was thinking. "I suppose she could've dropped it. Could it have been knocked out of her hand or her bag when the arrow hit her?"

He said, "If the police don't have it, I think a good search around the area might be productive. Sounds like an interesting timepiece."

"And if it doesn't turn up, I suppose that means someone stole it." Compared with murder, theft didn't seem very shocking, but there was something unspeakably vile about stealing from a dead woman.

CHAPTER 12

"A million pounds is a lot of money." I felt like I'd been saying those words a lot since the vampire knitting club meeting.

We were rattling along in the old Ford once again, headed toward Moreton-Under-Wychwood. I hadn't had such a great reception yesterday morning that I was thrilled to be driving back again, but I supposed Sylvia was right. If we were going to find out what was going on there, and clear Violet, Margaret Twig and me from suspicion, then we were going to have to go back to the scene of the crime.

"I suppose a million pounds is a lot of money to a mortal," Sylvia said in a rather bored tone, as though she measured her net worth in the billions. I was sure a million quid would be a lot to my Gran, who hadn't been a vampire long enough for the magic of compound interest to do its work.

I wondered, idly, how much Sylvia was worth. She must've made good money in the twenties when she was a stage and screen actress. From a couple of things she'd let slip, I got the feeling she'd been involved with some very generous, wealthy men in her time. But still, she'd only had a century to build her fortune, and she'd been through a couple of depressions.

Immediately my mind drifted to Rafe, who, as far as I could tell, had been around for about at least five centuries. I suspected his wealth would be astonishing. Naturally, they were all smart enough not to flash their money around. Well, Sylvia did have her Bentley and driver, and Rafe did inhabit a rather luxurious manor house, but they weren't conspicuous.

Keeping a low profile was an important part of staying safe for them. As it was for us witches. Until yesterday, I'd begun to believe it was more socially acceptable to be a witch these days. We weren't particularly secretive about our solstice events, and, while Margaret Twig didn't advertise with a sign out front of her cottage or anything, she was clearly in the habit of dispensing spells and potions to the paying public.

With a shiver, I realized how easily public opinion could turn once fear set in.

The good weather continued, and as I drove down the country road toward Moreton-Under-Wychwood, the trees arched overhead so the sunshine on the road ahead was dappled. Most of the ancient forest was gone, now, and between the trees were glimpses of green fields dotted with sheep.

Sylvia's cell phone rang. "It's Rafe," she said, as she picked up. Naturally, both Clara and I listened intently to Sylvia's side of the conversation, which was merely, "Oh, that is interesting. Yes, I'll tell her." She rang off. "He says no watch was found among Elizabeth Palmer's belongings. And he and Theodore and Hester came to the village green last night and searched the area where that woman was killed quite thoroughly. They didn't find a watch."

Which could mean everything or nothing. "That was kind of them, to take Hester."

"She's a dreadful pest, but she has sharp eyes," Sylvia said.

"And she does want to help," the much kinder Clara added.

We reached the outskirts of town and decided that our first port of call would be the coffee shop. Not only would there be hopefully some garrulous townspeople there, but I was frankly dying for coffee. The only problem with going for coffee with two vampires was I inevitably ended up discreetly drinking all three beverages.

Since it was a Monday morning, I had no trouble finding parking on the curb in front of the coffee shop. The three of us walked in and, unlike the day before, there were plenty of seats to be had. Still, partly, I suppose, because the three of us were thinking of protection, we drifted to a table near the back where no one was between us and the wall. However, unlike yesterday, the atmosphere was calm, verging on lethargic.

A few people checked us out, but they went back to their coffees and conversations or, in a couple of cases, their computers.

I went up to the coffee bar and ordered three small cappuccinos. I figured that would give me one and a half large, which would be a good hit of caffeine. I'd need it given how stressful this day was turning out to be. Thanks to two very controlling vampires, I'd be spending my morning questioning reluctant townsfolk and my afternoon questioning probably even more reluctant archers.

I put their coffees in front of Sylvia and Clara, and they both thanked me politely. Sylvia, always an actress, made a great show of adding a packet of raw sugar and vigorously stirring her drink. She knew how I liked my coffee. Clara was too busy looking around the room to get involved in amateur dramatics. She just left her coffee sitting in front of her. I drank mine down. It was a very good cup of coffee. Luckily.

I placed my empty cup quite near Clara, and when I was certain no one was looking, picked up her coffee and began to drink it. "Ask the barista if we can put up a poster advertising the knitting class in the window," Sylvia said in a low tone.

Between us, Theodore and I had concocted a simple poster, which I'd printed. I already had eighteen people signed up, but our plan was to take a flyer to Nora's as an excuse to ask her a bunch of nosy questions. Maybe I'd have been happier working today after all.

I pulled out one of the flyers, and as I stood, a woman came through the door whom I recognized. It was the woman who'd been running the white elephant stall where Elizabeth Palmer had bought a watch—one of her last acts before dying. I doubted anyone would murder someone over an old watch, but it was more than curious that the timepiece hadn't been among the murdered woman's things.

Since the lady from the white elephant was wearing a hand-knitted cardigan, I thought that would give me a good excuse to talk to her. The barista called out a cheerful, "Good morning, Mrs. Beasley. The usual?"

"Yes, please, Donnie."

"You sit down. I'll bring it out to you."

Clearly she was a regular. She sat at a table for four, so I suspected she was meeting someone. Before they arrived, I decided to make my move. I took the hastily created brochure and walked over to where she was sitting. She glanced up, squinting at me in surprise, clearly trying to recall where she'd seen me before.

I smiled. "I'm Lucy. I was helping with one of the booths at the fair on Saturday."

Her cheerful face grew grim, and a visible shudder went over her stout frame. "Oh my goodness, don't remind me of that dreadful day."

"You were running the white elephant."

"Yes." I decided to proceed carefully. First, I admired her cardigan. Like her, I was also wearing a hand-knitted garment, though Gran had made mine.

She brightened up at my compliment. "Thank you, dear. I

like the red. It's such a cheerful color. Especially when one is feeling a bit down in the dumps."

"I'm sure you don't need lessons, but since you obviously knit, I thought I'd let you know that we're starting a knitting class on Wednesday, here in town. I run Cardinal Woolsey's knitting and yarn shop in Oxford."

"Oh my, yes. I used to shop there. It's a lovely store. It was an older lady, I think, who had it."

"Yes. My grandmother. Sadly, she passed away, but she left the store to me, and I still run it."

"What a lovely way to honor your grandmother. What a shame she can't see you. She'd be so proud."

I was able to see almost every day exactly how proud my grandmother was of me, but of course, I didn't say that. I merely nodded, looking sorrowful.

She took the brochure and said that she thought it would be a good distraction to get out for an evening of knitting. "One can always learn something new."

I wasn't sure how to segue into immediately asking her questions about the white elephant until I had a brainwave. "I had planned to return to the white elephant when I got a break, but with that poor woman dying, of course, the fair ended abruptly."

"Oh, my dear, don't remind me. I put so much effort into that white elephant, too. I was hoping to raise so much money to rebuild the church steeple. It's falling to ruins, you know. I even cleaned out my own attic and went through old cupboards and drawers just so there'd be a few more interesting things for sale." She laughed suddenly. "My husband wasn't too pleased, though. Isn't it funny how years will go by and a man won't take any interest in something, and the minute it's gone, he wants it." She looked toward heaven.

I laughed too, feeling the hair rise on the back of my neck. "What, particularly, did he want back?"

"I don't know. A box full of bits and bobs. If old model soldiers and wooden toys were so precious to him, what were they doing shoved in an old box, I ask you?" We both laughed again.

"Where do most of your items come from?"

"They're all donated, of course. Local people get rid of unwanted items, and we put out the word to close-by communities. People drive in with things they no longer have use for. It's a great way to get some of the clutter out of our houses. Why do you ask?"

I scrambled to come up with a reason why I was being so nosy about her white elephant sale and grasped at a particularly unpalatable straw. "There was a lamp I liked. It was shaped like a poodle. That wasn't one of yours, was it?"

She looked at me as though I might've taken leave of my senses. "The poodle? Yes. I remember now. You looked at it before the fête even opened."

"Yes," I said brightly. "I thought it was humorous and kind of retro." I took a breath. "Also, there was a silver pocket watch. I saw it, but didn't have time to look closely. Do you remember it?"

She shook her head. "No. But I had volunteers help me get everything out of boxes and out on display. I didn't see everything."

I continued, "Is there perhaps a list of which items came from which people?"

"No." She brightened up, though. "But fortunately for you, I know exactly where that lamp is. I packed everything up at home and put the boxes away in our garden shed, ready for next year. I know exactly where that poodle lamp is. I can get it out for you today."

"That's wonderful," I said with false enthusiasm. "I'll make a nice donation to the church restoration fund."

"That's very sweet of you. It's nice to see items find a nice new home."

Oh, lucky me. She waved to two ladies who were coming in the door, and so I rose to leave. She said, "Give me your mobile number, and as soon as I've unpacked it, I'll give you a ring."

I thanked her, gave her my mobile number and told her I'd be in town for another couple of hours.

The barista gave us permission to put a poster in the window, and then Clara and Sylvia and I got ready to leave. First, of course, I had to pay a visit to the washroom to give back some of those three coffees I'd just drunk. By the time I came out, Sylvia and Clara both had their large hats on. As I walked past Mrs. Beasley's table, I sent her a quick wave, and she responded by putting her hand up to the side of her face, thumb up and baby finger extended in the classic *I'll call you* gesture.

We stepped into the June sunshine. As we ambled up the street, Sylvia turned to me. "Lucy, I can't believe you're interested in a poodle lamp. I didn't know where to look. I thought you had some modicum of taste, though it's difficult to tell, since you won't get rid of that sentimental junk of your grandmother's that's clogging up your flat."

"And your cat won't be too pleased to have a dog lamp in the house," Clara added.

I'd leave Sylvia's criticisms about Gran's belongings for another time. Mostly because I knew she was right. But how could I hurt Gran's feelings that way? She'd left me her collection of Victorian dolls, and every time she came into the flat, I thought she checked on them.

She'd be so upset if I put them away. Anyway, it wasn't like I had a lot of time for home decorating between running a shop and getting dragged into other people's business.

Being a witch was like having a second job.

I had to defend myself about the lamp, though. "Of course I

don't want the poodle lamp. It's the ugliest lamp in the history of illumination. It was the only excuse I could think of to ask questions about her white elephant sale."

Sylvia looked slightly mollified. "I'm pleased to see you have some sense. If you ask me, Agnes's dolls should go in a white elephant sale."

I might've defended myself more except I spied Nora heading into the small grocery store across the street. I suggested Sylvia and Clara see about getting a poster put on the community board in the village green, because this was my chance to talk to Nora. I didn't think we'd have a very intimate chat with two nosy vampires listening in on every word.

"We'll do that, and then we'll go into the post office to get out of the sun. We'll see if they'll put up a poster," Sylvia said.

The co-op wasn't large, but it was fiercely air-conditioned. I shivered as I entered. Not wanting to seem as though I was stalking Nora, I grabbed a green plastic basket and thought I might as well stock up on a few things since I was here. I was low on coffee, and the way my stress levels were lately, I needed more butter and powdered ginger and molasses for the cookies Gran kept turning out.

Apart from choosing groceries, I hoped to pick up a few clues.

CHAPTER 13

I caught up with Nora in the aisle devoted to smoked salmon, olives, pickles, dips and spreads.

Nora seemed confused by the selection of olives, which ranged from Greek through Italian to every stuffing imaginable. A person could spend their whole day trying to pick out an olive.

I reached for a packet of smoked salmon. It was a good snack to keep around for when I had an unexpected vampire visit, which was pretty much every day. I started in fake surprise and said, "Nora?"

She glanced at me and blinked in puzzlement.

"It's Lucy. We met at the fortune-telling booth at the village fête."

Her eyes widened, and she took a step back as though a witch had said "Boo" right in her face. She dropped the tub of Sicilian olives and hastily picked them up off the floor. Why was I making her so nervous?

"Your cousin," she said. Then silence stretched. "I heard Madame Violetta was your cousin." She inched away. "Why would she do something like that? We've always lived here so peacefully."

I didn't like either the fear in her eyes or where this conversation seemed to be heading. I was the one sleuthing. I didn't appreciate being looked at in that accusing fashion. "What, exactly, are you trying to say about my cousin Violet?"

She glanced up and down the aisle, but we were the only two there. She said, "Everyone knows Violet is a—" She waved her hand about as though that would define what she meant.

"Violet is a what?" I wasn't going to make this easy for her, even though I felt a niggle of fear under my breastbone. Fear that the witches in this area were being blamed.

"There's a rumor that she's a witch."

"Why is that a problem?"

"Look. Maybe she should move to Glastonbury or somewhere they're more comfortable with pagans. We're all regular people here." She leaned closer and her voice grew shrill. "Every fortune she gave that day came true. That can't be coincidence."

No. I would call it arrogance. Hubris even. I felt a surge of anger against Violet. She'd pulled us all into danger with her fortune-telling and made herself too easy a target.

However, if I were the murderer, I'd put a lot of effort into shifting the blame onto some poor witch as well. I was not so easily distracted, especially as I knew Vi hadn't killed anyone. So did Nora. "You know she couldn't have killed anyone. You were with her when Elizabeth Palmer died."

She looked at me as though I were incredibly naïve. "Witches have magical powers. She could easily have killed Elizabeth with a spell."

I felt like telling Nora Betts that magic wasn't nearly as easy as she seemed to think. I could barely manage simple spells. Witches were born with power and talent, but, as I was finding out the hard way, we had to practice and study. Frankly, it was exhausting work. Like being born a great violin virtuoso. How on earth would you even know until you picked up a violin?

I couldn't imagine being able to kill someone with magic when I wasn't even near them.

I decided to change tack, since this conversation wasn't getting us anywhere. "Elizabeth seemed like a great person. I remember how excited she was about her twenty-fifth anniversary cruise."

Nora's antagonism faded, and her eyes filled with sudden tears. "She was."

"I think I heard that you and your husband were going too?"

Nora's wet eyes widened. I wasn't sure whether it was because she was startled that I'd heard about her and her husband being invited along on the twenty-fifth anniversary cruise or whether she had picked up some tone in my voice that suggested a certain insensitivity in their tagging along.

"Yes. The four of us have been such great friends for so many years, they just couldn't imagine celebrating without us. Of course, my husband and I will be celebrating our twenty-fifth in a couple of years, and we'd planned another foursome event." A woman rolled her cart down the aisle, and we both flattened ourselves against the wall of olives. It was as obvious as that cart rattling down the aisle that the four of them would not be going on any celebrations together ever again.

"I hope you had cancellation insurance," I said, to keep the conversation going.

She reached almost at random for a plastic tub of hummus. "The three of us are still going on the cruise."

"You are?" I couldn't help the shock that emerged clear and sharp in my tone.

She put the hummus back and picked up one that was red, presumably from roasted red peppers. "We talked about it, and we all agreed. It's what Elizabeth would have wished." She shot me a quick glance. "Perhaps it sounds callous. But we decided to turn the cruise into a kind of a memorial voyage for Elizabeth. We'll take her ashes with us and have a small ceremony and say our goodbyes."

Her voice grew husky. "It will be a burial at sea."

She laughed, a sad little sound. "Elizabeth will finally get her anniversary cruise. Even if she is in an urn."

Okay, maybe she wasn't quite as insensitive as I had thought. Still, how much fun would Jason have on the cruise when his wife wasn't sharing the bed next to them, but packed inside a box ready to be tossed over the side?

"How is Jason holding up?"

Her hostility instantly returned. "How do you think he's holding up? He's just lost his wife in horrible circumstances."

"At least he's got good friends."

"He does."

I remembered the brochures in my bag and pulled one out. "I know you just lost your friend, but if you're looking for distraction, we're offering knitting classes here on Wednesday night. There's a beginner option and a more advanced pattern. Quite a few of the women here have expressed interest. Be great to have you."

She took the flyer. "Honestly, I'm not sure I'll feel up to it."

"Of course. Whatever you decide. I'm so sorry for your loss."

As I turned away, I saw her wipe her eyes with her free hand.

Coming out of the frigid grocery store into the bright sun was a shock. Not seeing my vampire friends in the village green, I crossed the street to the post office, which doubled as a stationery store. It looked like there were photocopiers and an Amazon pickup location there as well. I walked in and found Clara and Sylvia perusing the birthday cards. I wondered whether vampires kept celebrating their birthdays. Did you really want a card that said "Happy 589th"?

FAIR ISLE AND FORTUNES

Besides, would they celebrate the day they were actually born or the day they were turned into a vampire? It seemed fraught with complications to me. Then I realized my own birthday was coming up in a couple of weeks. Were they looking for birthday cards for me?

A year ago, on my twenty-seventh birthday, I was still with Todd the Toad and working in a cubicle in Boston. A mere twelve months later, I was living in Oxford, running a knitting shop—oh yeah, and a practicing witch. Some of my best friends were vampires.

Sometimes I looked at my life and wondered if I was crazy.

Vampires have more acute hearing than humans, so I was surprised they hadn't heard me, but then I realized they were having a low-voiced argument. My hearing wasn't vampire-acute, but it was better than most mortals'. I heard Clara say to Sylvia, "I think a surprise party would be delightful. She'll never expect it."

Sylvia shook her head. "That's exactly the problem with a surprise party. If one is going to be the center of attention, one wants to be looking one's best. There's the hair and makeup, the dress and shoes. The right jewelry. It all takes time, Clara."

I hid my smile and backed away so they wouldn't know I'd overheard them. I didn't care how much advance notice I had about a birthday party, I was never going to look as well turned-out as Sylvia. But I loved that the pair of them were trying to give me the best birthday possible.

I came around the corner a second time, calling out, "Sylvia? Clara?" By the time I reached them, they'd moved over to the sympathy cards. Clara looked up and said, "Lucy. We were wondering about a sympathy card for the grieving husband."

I felt slightly alarmed. "He doesn't even know you."

Sylvia shook her head. "Not from us. From you." She held up a hand. "And before you say he doesn't know you either, your excuse is that you were probably the last person to see his wife alive or at least to speak to her, and you thought you'd visit to bring him comfort. You can tell him how excited she was about their anniversary cruise. No need to mention Violet's fortune."

If the gossip about him and Nora was true, his girlfriend would have told him about Violet's warning that Elizabeth stay away from water. However, the idea wasn't a bad one. "So instead of mailing the card, you think I should take it to his home? Or the car dealership?"

"Yes. But take a very strong protection charm with you. He is the most likely culprit in his wife's death."

I wasn't sure how I felt about this idea. Barging in on a grieving husband was terrible. Barging in on a murderer was even worse. I seemed torn between the inappropriate and the life-threatening.

Before I could debate the idea of pushing my company on a grieving widower, my phone buzzed. "This is Florence Beasley, from the white elephant sale. Good news! I've unpacked that poodle lamp and even given it a bit of a dust to shine it up." It might be good news to her, but it was dreadful news to me. Why hadn't I noticed something else at that white elephant? Something I might actually want? With fake enthusiasm, I told her how happy I was.

Florence Beasley told me that her home was on Church Lane, which was, of course, behind the beautiful old stone church. Sylvia and Clara said they could keep themselves busy while I picked up that lamp. I didn't feel like moving the car yet again, so I decided to walk. I went around the edge of the green, not wishing to cross that bridge again and be reminded of poor Elizabeth Palmer lying there.

The church grounds were beautiful, and so, instead of walking around the church as I had planned, I opened the gate into the graveyard. Some of the gravestones were so old that time and weather had obliterated the writing, so I had no idea who lay beneath the crumbling stone, the buttercups and dandelions.

Others, however, were newer. In death, as in life, there was a hierarchy. Those with money in life had been more honored in death by ornate tombs overlooked by stone angels, while the more modest parishioners had nothing but a small square of stone to mark their passing.

A couple of the gravestones were recent enough that I wondered if Elizabeth would be buried here. Though not, I supposed, if she were going to be buried at sea. Someone had been busy cleaning the area around a newer gravestone. The dirt was freshly dug up, and a burst of flowers brightened the gray stone. I dawdled, hoping against hope that in the few minutes it would take me to reach Mrs. Beasley's house, someone else would realize how very much they wanted that poodle lamp and I would arrive to find it already sold. It was a faint hope, but it was all I had.

I passed a newish-looking and particularly imposing tomb and stopped to read the words.

"But about that day or hour no one knows, not even the angels in heaven, nor the son, but only the father. Be on guard! Be alert! You do not know when that time will come." Mark 13:32 – 33.

Beneath that Bible verse was inscribed, *Grayson Timmins, beloved husband and father, taken before his time. 1931 to 1981.*

I stood there listening to the buzz of bees and the sweetness of birdsong. Grayson Timmins. That was the name of the man who had been murdered, presumably after walking in on a burglary.

The village seemed so peaceful, the graveyard most of all, but not everyone lying beneath my feet had gone to their final rest by dying of old age.

CHAPTER 14

I headed toward the gate that would let me out onto the other side of the graveyard when I felt a feeling, almost as though I were being tugged, and I turned to see a large stone, obviously old and dingy with time and moss. A small plaque beside it said this was believed to be the grave of a witch, Ginnie Barrow, who'd been buried upside down and the heavy stone placed on top of her to prevent her from rising again.

I shuddered, thinking fear of witches was nothing new.

I opened the gate and shut it carefully behind me. As I looked around at the postcard-pretty village, I had the creepy feeling that I was being observed. I decided to pick up my poodle lamp and get out of here.

The first house on Church Lane was, of course, the vicarage. As I progressed, I noted that all the homes on the street were large. Number Twenty-Two was set at the end of the lane, behind imposing gates, so its many windows faced toward the church. Nothing about Florence Beasley had suggested she lived in a manor house, but this was easily the most imposing dwelling in town. A truck with the words Earthly Delights

Gardening written on the side was parked in the wide drive. It must take a staff of gardeners to keep up these grounds. One guy who looked barely out of his teens was mowing the lawn while an older man was stooped over, weeding.

I made my way to the front door and rang the bell. Mrs. Beasley answered the door, looking pleased to see me. "Lucy," she cried, as though we hadn't arranged to meet here only half an hour ago. "It's so good to see you." No doubt she thought I wouldn't come for that lamp after all and she'd be stuck with the thing.

"Your home is beautiful," I said.

She looked as though she had never received a compliment on the house before. She beamed. "I've always loved it. Of course, I can't take any credit. It was in my husband's family. Come in. I'll give you the tour."

It was impossible to resent her good fortune when she seemed surprised by it herself. The entrance hall was grand and imposing, featuring a large, carved wooden chest, heavy oil paintings in ornate frames and maroon wallpaper that had no doubt been the height of fashion when Queen Victoria was on the throne.

I took it all in and felt a bit like I'd stepped into a museum. "I see you love antiques."

She laughed. "It's lucky that I do, as my husband wouldn't hear of anything being changed. He was very close to his parents, you see, particularly his father, and he likes to keep the house exactly as he remembers it from his boyhood."

I liked the family sentiment, but I wondered how it would feel for her to be stuck in her husband's past. As though she had read my mind, she said, "Of course, our kitchen is modern, the sitting room is both modern and comfortable, and he finally let me redecorate the bedroom."

That seemed like a reasonable compromise. She led me through a formal living room that smelled of beeswax furniture

polish and felt curiously lifeless, as though not much enter-
taining went on there. The dining room could seat twenty
comfortably and again featured heavy furniture, including a
curio cabinet containing the strangest collection of things from
shells to old bottles to a few stuffed birds and then two rows of
fossils.

One painting on the wall was a still life, beautifully done I
was sure, but it would put me off my dinner if I was seated
across from it. It featured a sack with several dead birds
hanging out of it. I recognized the bright feathers of a pheasant,
and the other bird, its long neck draped across the canvas and
its eyes staring, looked like a heron. She followed my gaze. "It's
enough to put you off your dinner, I know. But the artist was
very famous, and those hunt scenes were more popular a
hundred years ago than they are today."

Over the fireplace in the dining room was a massive
portrait. The man in it looked like the lord of all he surveyed.
He had a heavy face, and even from the painting, his eyes were
arresting. He wore a dark suit, and in his hand was an open
pocket watch. Once more, she followed my gaze. "That was my
father-in-law. Sadly, I never met him. They say he was the most
punctual man. Always on time for everything, and he used to
write letters to the National Rail if ever the local train was so
much as a minute late." She shook her head. "The funny thing
is, my husband is exactly the opposite. Always late for
everything."

"It's a wonderful picture. You certainly get the feeling that
his personality was larger than life."

"Oh yes. People still talk about Grayson with enormous
respect."

It was funny that I'd just walked past the grave of a man
named Grayson. Perhaps it was a more common name here in
Moreton-Under-Wychwood than it was in the general popula-
tion. Then she said, "He met a tragic end. He came home one

day and surprised a burglar in the act of stealing from him. From what I've heard of my father-in-law, it's no surprise that he tackled that burglar head-on. Tragically for him, he was killed by the intruder."

I turned to her. "Your father-in-law was Grayson Timmins?" So it wasn't that common a name after all.

"Yes. Of course, it seems confusing, because our last name is Beasley. My husband was Grayson's wife's boy. They came here when Robert was five years old. Sadly, they never had children of their own, so Robert had no brothers or sisters. I often think it must've been rather lonely to be the only child in this large house, but luckily his memories are all happy ones."

I looked up again at that face. He didn't look like the kind of dad who'd carry a little kid on his shoulders and play football out in the back yard. But, I supposed, an oil painting couldn't tell everything about a man.

"Come into the kitchen. If you've time, I'll make you a cup of tea. I've got the lamp all ready for you. When I gave it a good rub, the pink really began to shine. It's in the kitchen."

Sadly, no one had rushed forward in the last few minutes to claim that lamp. It looked like I was going to be stuck with it. I didn't really want tea, but I did want to talk to Mrs. Beasley a little longer. "Sure. I'd love some tea. Do you mind if I look a little closer at the things in this curio cabinet?"

"Of course, dear. There are some very interesting fossils. Feel free to open the cabinet and take a closer look. Robert loves to show off his father's collection." She smiled at me. Warm and motherly. "I'll just put the kettle on. Come in whenever you're ready."

I waited until she'd left the dining room and then swiftly brought my phone out of my purse. That pocket watch in the painting looked an awful lot like the one Elizabeth had bought at the white elephant sale. Not that I was any expert on pocket watches, of course. Which was why I snapped a photograph.

First I took one that included the whole painting, and then I zoomed in on the watch itself. Naturally, the artist hadn't lavished a great deal of attention on that watch, but still I thought that vine pattern was similar to the one I'd seen in Elizabeth Palmer's watch.

I was going to peer more closely at the fossils in the cabinet just so I could tell Mrs. Beasley that I had admired them, but as I moved toward that cabinet, I felt as though I'd walked into a freezer. Goose flesh rose on my arms, and my heart began to pound. Fear and anger filled the air.

I wanted to move, but I felt frozen to the spot.

"Well, hello, there," a friendly male voice said from behind me.

It was as though someone had turned on the light, dispelling the darkness and the horror. I moved quickly to the side of the room, nearer the window. The man who'd spoken blinked, as though trying to place me. He was about my dad's age, I thought, which would put him close to fifty. He had a kind of vague way of looking at me that also reminded me of my dad, as though his brain were taken up with more important things than day-to-day conversation.

He wore gray sweats, his face was damp with perspiration, and he was huffing slightly. Call me a genius, but I had the feeling he was coming back from a run. Either that or about to have a heart attack.

"Hi," I said. "I'm Lucy. Your wife invited me to come and pick up an item I bought at the white elephant sale at the village fête."

"Oh. Right. Good."

The door from the kitchen opened, and Mrs. Beasley appeared. "Lucy?" Then she saw the man I'd been talking to, and her eyebrows flew up. "Robert! What are you doing still here? You're meant to be at the town meeting. I promised them faithfully you'd be on time today." She glanced at her watch and moaned. "Oh, you're so late."

Robert seemed blissfully unworried about the time. "They always chat a bit before the meeting. I'll just shower and be on my way."

"No. No shower. Towel yourself off and get going. Please, Robert. I promised."

"All right." He went back out of the room, then paused at the door and turned to me politely. "Very nice to have met you."

"You, too."

"Are you staying in the area?"

"Robert!"

"Right. On my way." But he seemed in no rush.

I followed her into the kitchen. Unlike the showrooms in the front of the house, the kitchen was like Mrs. Beasley herself, warm and homey. There was a big Aga stove against one wall, but she plugged an electric kettle into a wall socket.

"I love that man, but he'll be the death of me. No idea of time."

"Not like his father, then." The man had a verse about time on his gravestone, for heaven's sake.

"No. Not at all."

Following a hunch I asked, "Was that why the painter took such detail in painting Grayson Timmins's pocket watch? Because he was so punctual?"

"Yes, exactly."

"I'd love to see that watch. It looks beautiful."

She poured boiling water into a bright red teapot. "I'd love to see it, too," she said sadly. "But I'm afraid it was one of the items the burglar stole." She shook her head. "What kind of person could do such a thing? Kill someone and then take the watch right off their body?"

On another hunch, I asked, "Did Mr. Timmins die in that dining room?"

She shuddered. "How did you guess? Of course, the carpet was changed and the place was thoroughly cleaned, but I've never felt quite comfortable in that room."

Try being a witch. I could have told her exactly the spot where it had happened. Weirdly, the likeness of Grayson Timmins must have witnessed his murder. If only that picture could talk.

"It seems unthinkable, doesn't it? I took a shortcut through the graveyard, and I saw your father-in-law's tomb. Even the Bible verse talks about time."

"Yes. Robert's mother chose it. It seemed appropriate. Robert said they'd have buried his watch with him if they'd got it back."

And yet, someone had taken that pocket watch. I was very much afraid that it had disappeared again when Elizabeth Palmer was killed.

Why? What was so special about that watch, and did it somehow link the two murders?

CHAPTER 15

*C*lara had said she would drive Gran's car and drop me off at Rafe's for my second appointment of the day, a visit to the Wychwood Bowmen. She assured me she was an excellent driver, as she'd driven trucks and ambulances in the war. "If I could manage to steer an ambulance through the rubble-strewn streets of London, carrying wounded Blitz victims in the back, I think I can manage to drive this car safely for a few miles."

Clara squeezed herself into the driver's seat with Sylvia beside her, and I was left to wedge myself into the back seat with a shiny pink poodle lamp as my companion. Clara pulled away from the curb, and while she did deliver us to Rafe safely, she drove as though we were roaring along through the London Blitz dodging bombs. Actually, I wondered how any wounded had survived the trip to the hospital, the way she changed gears with such force that I ended up clutching the lamp to stop it from breaking. Though that might've improved it.

However, at length she deposited me at the top of Rafe's circular drive, and apart from some fear that I might need dental work, I was in one piece. So, unfortunately, was the lamp.

In order for me to get out, Clara had to get out too and fold back the seat.

By that time, Rafe's butler or manservant or whatever he was had the double doors open to the Georgian manor house.

He said, "Good morning, Lucy. Can I offer you some coffee?"

He must've seen the look of revulsion on my face. More coffee or tea, I did not need. I was so jittery from caffeine, I felt like my fingernails were vibrating. "Morning, William. Maybe just some water?" I asked

"Of course." I pretended I didn't hear the screech as Clara roared off down the drive, spitting gravel behind her. Even Henri the peacock stopped preening long enough to glance up. He looked particularly handsome today, the sun glinting off his iridescent blue-green feathers. "Do you mind if I walk around the grounds a bit?"

"Of course not. It's a beautiful day. I'll tell Rafe you're here, and I'll bring you out your water. Would you like anything to eat?"

I felt bad. He must have so few people to cook for. Rafe was certainly low-maintenance in the food department. And it was nearly lunchtime, after all. "Maybe a sandwich?"

He looked so pleased, I was glad I'd asked. "I can offer you lox and cream cheese. Ham and cheese? Steak tartare?" I glanced at him and saw his eyes were dancing with amusement. No doubt that was what his boss most often ordered.

"Ham and cheese would be great."

I walked carefully toward the peacocks. There were three of them. The one I was fairly certain was Henri was out front, plump and pleased with himself. He all but posed in front of a white rose bush. Two other peacocks were pecking the ground beneath a clump of bright red peonies. On the other side of the drive, the peahens were going about their business. I wondered if they minded being so much less glamorous than their male counterparts or even noticed.

I walked carefully so as not to startle Henri, and he watched me steadily out of his black, beady eyes. When I drew closer, I crooned to him, "What a handsome boy you are." He really was, too. Sleek and clearly well-fed. To my astonishment, he put his head to one side and then the other, and then, as I watched, his glorious tail opened out into a perfect iridescent fan. And then he danced for me, turning in a complete circle, his fanned tail waving slightly, reminding me of a showgirl's headdress in Vegas. Though, presumably, peacocks had the idea first.

I giggled in delight and clapped my hands. I pulled out my phone and took a picture. Then I took a video as he did his whole routine again, twirling slowly around. "Oh, you are a beauty."

Behind me a low, amused voice said, "He's flirting with you. It's mating season, and I think Henri has a crush."

I turned to see Rafe watching me from under the shade of an apple tree. I felt a little foolish that I'd been caught crooning to a bird. Since our kiss, I felt a little foolish altogether around Rafe.

He was, as always, cool and elegant. He wore black linen trousers and a white cotton shirt open at the neck. Conscious of the sun, I said, "Should we go inside?"

He shook his head. "William is serving lunch on the patio." He held out his hand. "Come."

I put my hand into his cool one, and he led me around his stone manor house via a path through more gardens. Behind the manor was a beautiful, well-shaded stone patio that looked out over the grounds. Beyond the gardens were acres of rolling green and the glint of a lake, around which fat, happy-looking sheep munched on grass.

William came out with my sandwich served on a beautiful china plate as well as a jug of ice water. He'd also added a cold salad of sliced tomatoes, fresh mozzarella and fragrant basil leaves, all drizzled with olive oil and balsamic vinegar. On the tray was a thermos flask for Rafe, and we settled companionably enough to our lunch.

Rafe even helped himself to a little of the cold salad. "How's Violet holding up?" he asked me.

"She's pretty shaken up. That attack on her house really threw her. She claims she's being shunned when she goes into the village. I'm sure it's all in her mind, but still that can't be pleasant."

"What did you discover in the village this morning? Did your plan to visit Nora Betts work out?"

I related my conversation with Nora. "It seems so crass and tacky of them to go on the cruise, but maybe it does make sense to turn it into a burial at sea and scatter her ashes. I don't know."

He looked out over the fields. "If someone I loved had died, I'm not sure I could go on a trip we'd planned together." I wondered whether he'd ever been in that situation. In all his time on earth, he must have loved and lost, but I was becoming a little better at keeping my mouth shut and my thoughts to myself.

"I feel the same, but I suppose we're all different. I didn't even have to go to her house. She walked into the grocery store, and I followed her. It seemed like fate was offering us a break. But fate was only toying with me. As usual."

His lips quirked at that. It was nice to know one of the sexiest men I'd ever met found me amusing.

"All I found out is that there are people in the village who think Violet killed Elizabeth Palmer by witchcraft. And that she and her husband are still going on that cruise with the recent widower."

As I considered the way fate kicked me around like its plaything, I added, "Oh, and I'm now the owner of a very large, very shiny, very pink lamp shaped like a poodle."

"I had no idea the shopping was so good in Moreton."

So then I had to tell him how I'd come by the lamp and how I'd visited Grayson Timmins's home and seen his portrait with the watch. "I'm almost certain it's the one Elizabeth Palmer bought at the white elephant sale."

As soon as I finished lunch, we headed out to the Wychwood Bowmen in the Range Rover. The smooth, quiet ride was a pleasure after Clara. We drove through narrow country roads with little traffic. He seemed to know the way, so I relaxed and enjoyed the scenery. At length, we turned into a narrow lane and finally ended up in a gravel parking lot by a squat building that sort of looked like a large shoebox, behind which stretched a very long field with straw bales and archery targets. We had arrived at the home of the Wychwood Bowmen.

There were about a half dozen cars already there. Most looked to be fairly recent models of mid- to high-end cars. We got out and trudged to the entrance. Inside, it looked like clubhouses everywhere. Lino on the floor, industrial lighting, a counter with a cash register and bulletins hanging from the walls. A large sign announced the rules of the club, and on another was a price list.

Behind the counter, a man was bent over fiddling with what I thought was an arrow tip. He glanced up when we entered and then, seeing we were strangers, put down the arrow. "Afternoon."

"Good afternoon," Rafe and I echoed.

"How can I help you?"

Rafe went up and explained that we were interested in taking up archery and possibly joining the club.

He looked at us as though assessing our strength and fitness. He was in his forties, I thought, with a prematurely wrinkled face, perhaps from squinting at targets in the sunshine. "Well, you've come to the right place. Do you have any experience?"

He looked to me first. "I did some archery at summer camp. That was like ten years ago."

He nodded and turned to Rafe, who put out his hands. "It's been years."

I had a feeling by years, he meant centuries.

The man said, "Well, let's get you set up and head out to the back, and I'll give you a few tips. The price for our 'have a go' session is twenty pounds each. If you like it, we've got a beginner's class starting next week. We've got a few couples already signed up."

I stiffened when he said the word couple, but Rafe said that sounded fine and dug out his wallet.

"I imagine safety is very important," I said. "I'm a little nervous to go out there."

The archery guy shot me a glance that would have run me through if there'd been an arrow attached to it. "I suppose you're referring to the incident over the weekend?"

Nice of him to head straight to where I wanted to go. "Yes. I admit I was nervous coming here today."

He shook his head. "None of us can work out how that terrible tragedy occurred. But I can assure you we take safety very seriously. Very seriously indeed."

While Rafe paid and filled out a form, I wandered over to the glass display case. Inside were various arrows and leather gloves, things that no doubt brought joy to the heart of archery enthusiasts. Perhaps as encouragement, they had displayed a list of club champions. It seemed the club competed locally and nationally. I ran my eye casually down the list of names and stifled a gasp. The third from the top, the club champion of three years ago, was Jason Palmer. Jason Palmer, who'd been about to lose everything when the untimely death of his wife promised an extremely fat life insurance policy that would solve all his financial problems.

Violet had foreseen that crossing water would end in death for Elizabeth. I wondered if he'd originally intended to push his wife overboard on their anniversary cruise. Something had pushed that plan forward to Saturday. Were his creditors closing in? Had Nora called to tell him about Violet's fortune and that his wife was planning to cancel the cruise? Was that what got him scuttling up to the top floor of the village hall with a hastily pilfered arrow? This theory meant that not only had Elizabeth's husband wanted her dead, but also her best friend.

Or maybe Jason Palmer had planned the arrow caper all along. He certainly hadn't been around when his wife was killed. Every other person in the village seemed to have been at the fête except him.

I snapped a hasty photo of the championship board and then went to refresh my archery skills. I needed the refresher, but Rafe clearly didn't. He fumbled and hit his first arrow outside the target range, so it buried itself in the hay bale, but as soon as the guy who'd shown us the ropes went back inside the clubhouse, he hit the bull's-eye again and again. It was a pleasure to watch him, so smooth and focused.

I didn't do too badly, either, considering how long it had been.

I waited until we were back in the Range Rover to say to Rafe, "Did you see the champion board in the display case?" Since I knew he hadn't, I continued, "Jason Palmer was club champion three years ago."

CHAPTER 16

*H*e backed the car out smoothly. "And Jason Palmer definitely had the most to gain in his wife's death."

"I wonder if the police know all this."

"If they don't, they soon will. It's not a difficult trail to follow."

In other words, "Don't interfere, Lucy." Since I suspected he was right, I didn't argue. That didn't mean we wouldn't continue our own investigation.

"I wish I could get to Elizabeth's husband somehow, but I don't want to show up on his doorstep with a casserole. I'm not a neighbor or a friend."

Rafe said, "There's nothing easier."

I'd discovered that Rafe's idea of easy and mine were not always the same. I pushed my hair over my shoulder. "I am not breaking into the man's house in the middle of the night, if that's what you had in mind."

He got that expression he often gets when he's looking at me, as though he's trying not to laugh at me. "I don't know where you get these notions about me, Lucy. I was only going to suggest that you take a trip out to his car dealership."

I banged myself upside the head, but softly so I didn't do any damage. "That is such a great idea. I can't believe I didn't think of it. Of course, I'll pretend I'm in the market for a new car."

He gave me that look again. "No offense to your current automobile. That was a fine set of wheels in 1987. But perhaps you should be in the market for a new car."

He was right, of course, but the advantage of Gran's old car was that I wasn't too worried about banging it up or denting it while I navigated fiendishly narrow lanes on the wrong side of the road. If I bought a brand-new car? I'd spend the whole time waiting for some sneaky rock wall from medieval times to reach out and scratch up my car. Also, with Gran's old heap, I didn't have to make car payments. "I'll take a look."

Rafe said, "Excellent. I'll come with you."

I felt a little huffy. "You don't think a woman can buy her own car?"

"I'd like to get a glimpse of Mr. Jason Palmer. That's all." He put his hands up in a very placating way. "I'll even let you drive us there."

I glared at him. "I may be a feminist, but I'm not a fool. If you drive us there in an expensive Range Rover, he'll take us more seriously. If I show up in that old beater, he'll pawn me off on the lowliest salesperson."

He didn't argue with me because we both knew I was right. He started to put the coordinates into his GPS.

"What, now?"

"Why not?"

"I feel like I should prepare for meeting Elizabeth's probable killer. Think of biting, incisive questions to ask him."

"You can do that in the car."

There was no point arguing since we were on our way.

Moreton Motorcars was located in an industrial park a couple of miles from Moreton-Under-Wychwood. It looked as though the industrial park had grown up around it. Rafe didn't turn the car into the dealership right away. Instead, he cruised slowly past it and then around the block. "He doesn't have much inventory," he said.

As we came around in front of the car lot again, I could see what he meant. It didn't look as though business was thriving. There were maybe a dozen cars in the whole lot, which had room for many more times that. I glanced over at Rafe. "We already know his business is in trouble."

"Critical if he can't even get inventory to sell. Or else business is so brisk, he can't keep cars in stock. Be interesting to find out which."

We barely got out of the car before a man was coming out of the squat building to greet us. I recognized him from the coffee shop. He was pulling on his suit jacket lapels as though he had just shoved himself into the jacket. A metal nameplate on his pocket informed us that he was Jason Palmer, general manager. I'd worried that we'd be greeted by a junior salesperson, but, as far I could tell, Jason Palmer was the only salesperson on the lot.

As he walked toward us with his hand held out, I could see him swiftly run his eyes over me. I didn't think he was assessing my financial ability to buy a car. I thought he was checking me out. I wouldn't call him good-looking as much as someone who'd been good-looking. He had the rugged good looks of a rugby player, with a muscular body and a tough-guy face, sporting a nose that had obviously been broken at some point. He'd lost most of his hair and, perhaps to compensate, his face had that stubbly unshaven look. His eyes were dark brown and, while he didn't appear broken by tragedy, he definitely looked as though he wasn't getting enough sleep.

His grip was firm without being bone-breaking as he introduced himself, and he quickly transferred his hand from mine to Rafe's. He gestured to the Range Rover. "That's a nice ride you've got there. Are you thinking of trading it in?"

"No," Rafe said. "It's Lucy who's in the market for a new car."

He turned back to me. "Excellent. You've come to the right place. Our prices are competitive, and our after-purchase service is exemplary."

The three of us looked around at the dozen or so cars in the lot and Rafe said, "You seem a bit low on stock."

He shook his head as though surprised himself that there were so few cars that I might buy. "You know how it is. As soon as I get them, they're sold. There's a waiting list right now for several models, but if you order something today, I can have it delivered within a few weeks."

"That would be fine," I said.

He rubbed his hands together, and his wedding ring flashed in the sunlight. I was struck by a pang of sadness for his poor wife, who had been so looking forward to their silver anniversary trip. "Now, did you have anything special in mind?"

Well, if I was going to waste my time on a car lot, I might as well look at some cars. "I definitely want something small and easy to drive, and I prefer an automatic if you have one." I was really struggling with Gran's stick shift.

He put a finger up in the air as though he were conjuring a rabbit out of a hat. "I think I have exactly the right thing for you. Come right this way."

He led me to a small white car with enough room in the back seat for two adults to sit in comfortably and a roomy hatchback. In spite of myself, I was impressed. It was exactly the kind of thing I would look at if I were in the market for a car.

He rambled on about fuel efficiency and comfort ratings until I finally and rather bluntly asked the price. The initial fantasy I'd had of driving home in a brand-new car was immediately dispelled. He must've seen my face fall, for he said, "Of course, this is a higher-end model. You can order a base model and, of course, we have some excellent payment plans on approved credit."

I was about to tell him I couldn't afford it when Rafe said, "Let's take it for a test drive."

Of course, I knew he was just stretching out our time so that we could ask Jason those searching questions about the death of his wife, but still, I felt guilty driving a car I couldn't afford. The man went and got the keys and returned in a couple of minutes. He was clearly going to come with us. "Is it all right to leave your office empty like that?"

He looked back as though surprised that there was no one here but himself. "It's all right. One of my colleagues will be back any minute now."

Whatever. I got in the driver's seat, and Jason got in beside me, while Rafe squeezed himself into the back. I felt incredibly nervous driving a brand-new car down narrow country lanes on what I still considered the wrong side of the road. However, every amateur detective had their challenges. I started the engine on the first try, unlike Gran's car, which immediately gave me a burst of confidence. I adjusted the mirrors to my liking, and then we set off.

In truth, it was a pleasure to drive a car that had a lot less personality than Gran's. It did what I wanted it to do without struggle or argument. Jason seemed content for me to get to know the vehicle on my own. He said, "I haven't seen you before. Do you live in the area?"

I told him that I lived in Oxford and ran a wool shop.

Rafe asked whether the struggling economy was affecting his business. I thought it was rather a blunt question, but Jason didn't take offense. He said, "I never give in to negative thinking. My position is that people need cars. They need to get around. I provide better prices than most, better service than most, and I've built up extremely good loyalty so most of my customers are repeat business."

I thought that was a very impressive answer. But was it true?

I braked in order to let a goose cross the road, and that made me laugh. "It must be wonderful living in the country. Especially in a lovely village where everyone knows everyone else."

He made a rude kind of snorting noise. "And where everyone knows everyone else's business. It's taken me a long time to get used to village life. I'm from London, you see, a city of eight million strangers."

"What brought you to Moreton-Under-Wychwood?" I asked. It was exactly the sort of question you would ask a stranger.

"My wife's from here." And he cleared his throat. "Was from here, I should say. I recently lost her."

"I'm so sorry," I said, and I meant it. I hated to do this, but it was possible he'd killed her, and I'd come to ask tough questions, after all. "Was she ill?"

"No. It was an accident." Then the words seem to burst out of him. "Some fool shot her with an arrow at the village fête."

"What?" I asked in barely-simulated shock. Even though I'd been there, it still shocked me. What a crazy way to die.

"The police are investigating, of course, but they haven't caught the bas—the killer yet. They must have run away when they realized what they'd done."

"You mean someone shot your wife by accident?"

"Oh, yes. Lizzie didn't have an enemy in the world. It was a bored teenager who only planned to cause panic, I'm sure. Not to kill anyone."

"That's an awfully dangerous prank."

He nodded and didn't say anything. I thought he was struggling with emotion and, since the goose had now crossed to the other side of the road, I rolled smoothly forward in the car. I didn't drive it for long, and I was very happy to return it unscathed. Then he escorted us inside and brought out a glossy brochure. He clipped his business card to it and then asked for my name and phone number. I hated to give it to him, but I knew he was only doing his job. As we drove away in the Range Rover, I felt that we'd sort of wasted his time. "I thought we'd learn more."

Rafe didn't answer for a moment and then said, "I think we learned a great deal."

"Like what? That the newest model has a state-of-the-art fuel-saving economy feature?"

"No. That Theodore was right and Jason Palmer is in serious financial trouble." He took one hand off the wheel and stuck his index finger in the air. "Number one. Very few cars in the lot." He held up another finger. "Number two. There were no employees."

"He said his colleague would be back soon," I reminded Rafe.

"Did you see another desk that showed any signs of human habitation?" He shook his head and answered his own rhetorical question. "He has no staff. No colleagues. Also, while you were batting your big blue eyes at him and he was showing you all the features in that glossy brochure, I caught a glimpse of his electric bill. It's overdue. He's barely able to keep the lights on."

"That's bad."

"Nothing a million pounds won't fix."

I shuddered. "I can't bear to think that he would kill that lovely woman just for money."

"Well, somebody killed her for some reason. I think he's a very likely candidate."

I reminded him that it was while foretelling Nora's future that Violet had seen the hand writing that check.

"Then we have to assume that she's going to share in the windfall. And perhaps deserves a share of the blame."

"What do you think of his theory that it was a teenage prank gone wrong?"

"I think Jason Palmer needs to come up with a better story if he's going to stay out of jail."

CHAPTER 17

ednesday evening found me and Sylvia and Clara back in Moreton-Under-Wychwood for the first knitting class. There was a reason the phrase "close-knit community" had become a cliché. I'd discovered that people who liked to knit and crochet also liked to hang around together, as evidenced by the fact that we'd had more than twenty knitters and novice knitters sign up.

I dropped Sylvia and Clara at the farmhouse and then turned back to town. Joanna was providing tea and coffee, but I thought I'd run into the grocery store and pick up some cookies. I had come early in order to set up for the evening.

I wanted this evening to go well, not only for snooping, but for my business. I had quite a few orders that had either been phoned in to the shop or ordered online. I needed to think about doing more of these. Gran had, as usual, been delighted at anything that improved business for Cardinal Woolsey's and also, as usual, was disappointed that she couldn't be part of the knitting classes. My poor Gran. She so wanted to be part of a knitting shop again. In fifty years or so, when all her current clients were dead or had ceased to remember her, she could come back and run Cardinal Woolsey's again. But until then, she had to find something to keep herself busy. In my heart of hearts, I knew she was going to have to move on from Oxford. But we both knew that I still needed her. I relied on her advice and her experience, and I knew that she loved having me around.

As I came out of the co-op, I almost bumped into Ian Chisholm about to enter. He had his work outfit on—suit, shirt and tie—and he wore his serious, all business expression. When he saw me, his face broke into a smile and then melted into a look of confused embarrassment. Ian had messed up with me, and he knew it. We'd had a few dates and seemed to be heading toward a relationship, but between his busy case-work and getting a foolish crush on someone else, though that was partly my fault, he'd screwed things up. Or we both had.

We made awkward, embarrassed small talk. "Lucy. What a surprise." Then a pause. "It's so good to see you."

Now it was my turn. "Ian. Nice to see you, too."

It went on like that for a minute or two. Awkward jerky phrases that barely covered a mass of confusion and misunder-standing. Finally, I asked him what he was doing in Moreton-Under-Wychwood. "I'm here on a case, actually."

I was puzzled. "I thought DI Thomas was heading the murder investigation."

He relaxed enough to give me his charming grin. "And, as usual, you seem to be right in the middle of the case. Yes, DI Thomas is investigating the murder of Elizabeth Palmer. But because of that suspicious death, we reopened a cold case. I'm investigating an unsolved murder that happened here thirty years ago."

I nodded. "I'd heard of that. So you think they're connect-ed." I was totally fishing here.

"No one knows for sure. But any time you have two suspi-cious deaths in a community this size, it's worth investigating."

I thought of the nice ladies gathered in Joanna's farmhouse. "Is there any danger?"

"To the other residents of Moreton-Under-Wychwood, you mean?"

"Yes. And people who come from Oxford to teach knitting classes. For instance."

"I don't think so. Though, from what I'm hearing, there are a couple of women here who seem to be suffering harassment. There are some old-fashioned superstitions around here about witchcraft. One of them is your assistant Violet."

I was surprised the cops knew about the witch angle. "Do you think I should invite Violet to stay with me until the trouble passes?" The last thing I needed was my bossy cousin Violet living with me. It was bad enough that we worked together.

Fortunately for me, he shook his head. "I think she's safe enough. But you might let her know you have a bed available in case things escalate."

I supposed it was the least I could do. I only hoped Margaret Twig wouldn't hear about my invitation and think it included her. Living with Violet would be bad enough. Living with Margaret Twig? When she moved into my flat, I'd be moving out.

It was in a thoughtful mood that I drove back to Joanna's farmhouse. I set up a table with all the orders on them and the purchasers' names.

Since I was becoming a savvier businesswoman than the girl who'd stumbled into Cardinal Woolsey's without a clue less than half a year ago, I had also brought a selection of patterns and wools, notions, and a few kits by Teddy Lamont, our most popular designer. We had twenty-three people registered, which was excellent, and I'd brought enough extra supplies that a few knitters could register at the door.

Sylvia seemed reasonably excited about taking center stage

once again. Maybe she wasn't playing a heroine of the silent screen, but at least she'd be getting some stage time. Always an actress at heart, she had dressed the part. Every part of her outfit that was visible was hand-knit, crocheted, or embroidered, right down to her embroidered slippers. She wore a black cashmere sweater inset with silver geometric shapes over hand-knit trousers made of the finest silk wool. I think she'd designed the slippers herself, as they were also black and silver and echoed the design in her sweater without copying it.

Her silver hair was perfectly coiffed, her makeup flawless, and diamonds glittered from her ears, around her neck and on her fingers.

She was as sharply elegant as Clara was comfortably frumpy. Her sweater was also hand-knitted, in bright green that she'd embellished with crocheted flowers. She wore a stretchy polyester skirt and black orthopedic shoes. Her gray hair was styled in pin curls, probably the way she'd worn it in the forties.

The students began arriving at six-thirty, half an hour before class began. They arrived in twos and threes, hardly anyone alone. They all seemed excited about having a class right in their village. Florence Beasley arrived with Hilary Beaumont, the officious woman who'd been running the fête. "And how's the lamp working out, Lucy?"

"Fine," I answered with a smile about as fake as the one painted on the poodle's face. I'd put it in the guest room, though I'd have to move it if I ever had a guest.

"This is a wonderful idea. It's really helping to bring the community together and get our minds off what happened at the fête."

She moved on, then, as Emily Bloom, the wife of the retired police officer, came in with another woman I vaguely recognized from the fête. As she took her package, I asked how her mother was.

She shook her head. "Not too well. Your fortune-teller was

right. Mother didn't want anyone to know how ill she was. She didn't want to go into a home, you see. Fortunately, I've been able to hire a nurse to look in on her every day. I'm only back for a day or two to take care of a few things and pack more clothes, then I'll head back for a longer visit." She sighed. "At least I'll have my knitting to keep me occupied."

Several people stopped to thank me and picked up their ordered merchandise and browsed the table.

Second in elegance to Sylvia was Joanna, who wore a blue and white dress that showed off toned arms. She offered tea and coffee and, as the women settled into chairs and couches, there was a happy buzz of conversation.

It was nearly seven, and I had very few unclaimed kits when Nora walked in. She looked bashful as she approached me. "I didn't register. I wasn't sure if I was going to come. Then I thought, Liz and I would've come together to something like this. I suppose I'd feel more lonely if I stayed home." She glanced at the chattering, giggling women already present. "Do you have room for me?"

I assured her that I did and set her up with one of the remaining kits. She chose the novice one.

As she was joining the others, the door opened again, and this time it was Dierdre Gunn, the woman whose budgie had died, coming in. She hadn't registered, either. She paused inside and glanced swiftly around. I thought she was looking for Violet or Margaret Twig. I was as swiftly trying to see whether she had that witch-exposing crystal with her, but if she did, she kept it hidden.

Good.

When she was satisfied that the venue was witch-free, she asked me if she could join the class. I wanted to say no, but Florence Beasley had already seen her and called out a greeting.

She chose the complicated pattern and as she paid said, "I need something to occupy my evenings now my Billy's gone."

I was pleased to see that this was a punctual bunch. By seven, everyone who'd registered was there, and Nora made twenty-five. At five past seven, Sylvia stood up and introduced herself and Clara. She gestured to me in a rather theatrical manner. "And, of course, you all know Lucy Swift, who runs the wonderful Cardinal Woolsey's knitting shop in Oxford."

After an awkward moment, everyone clapped and I nodded my head, still sitting at the back of the room. I was careful not to sit inside the knitting circle. If anyone got tangled up in their knitting, I didn't want them coming to me for help. I had my computer out and pretended I was doing something terribly important when really I was only checking email.

Sylvia was an excellent teacher, and Clara was the perfect assistant, happy to work one on one with any knitter who got in a muddle. After a while, the group of knitters began to multi-task, gossiping while they knitted.

"Did anyone else get a visit from the police?" Hilary Beaumont asked.

"Oh, yes," Dierdre Gunn answered. "Well, I told them Billy had died too, under strange circumstances."

There were murmurs of mingled sympathy and embarrassment.

"He was such a nice young fellow who came to see me. He told me he was sorry for my loss." Her knitting needles flashed as she continued, "Though they seemed more interested in anything I knew of Elizabeth Palmer." She definitely sounded put out that her budgie's death hadn't rated higher.

"What did you tell them?" Florence Beasley asked.

"Well, I didn't see anything that happened. I did tell them how I used to look after her when she was a girl and her parents went out of an evening. Oh, they doted on Elizabeth. So did I, really. She was such a sweet girl, just like a princess living in that lovely house. They wanted to know about Jason, too." She flipped her needles to start the next row. "But I couldn't tell them much. I didn't know him as well. I told them about that witch who cursed my Billy."

Florence Beasley said, "A nice young man came to see us only today. DI Chisholm. He's very good-looking." She fanned herself, and several of the women laughed. "He was trying to work out if there could be a connection between my father-in-law's death and that of Elizabeth Palmer." I waited, wondering if anyone had any ideas. Florence flattened her knitting on her lap to have a look at the first few rows. She said, "I told him it must have been someone from another town who killed Elizabeth, just like it was a random thief who attacked Grayson Timmins. I'm convinced of it, and so I told that nice inspector. No one in Moreton-Under-Wychwood would kill anyone. Why would they?"

Nora Betts stopped knitting to stare at her. "They would if they were witches."

CHAPTER 18

$\mathcal{T}$hursday, Violet and I had a busy day in the shop. She was distracted and rather moody, but it wasn't until near the end of the day that I found time to ask her what was wrong.

She tossed her hair over her shoulder and turned to glare at me. "What do you think is wrong? Half the villagers make the sign of the cross every time they see me. I'm completely out of bread and milk because people stare at me in the grocery store. And someone scrawled symbols all over my front gate."

I could imagine how unnerving this must be for her, so even though I didn't want to, I said, "Why don't you move in here for a week or two until things get sorted out? You know I've got a spare bedroom."

Her face softened. "That's nice of you, Lucy, thanks. My grandmother's offered to let me live with her, too, but I don't want to be chased out of my own house. Why should I leave? I haven't done anything wrong."

"I wish we could use our gifts to see who the murderer is."

"It doesn't work that way. You yourself know that magic is slippery and sometimes unpredictable. I can see glimpses of

131

the future, but I have to have the person in front of me, and they have to be cooperative. That's why the fortune-telling booth worked so well. My customers were very open to me, and so I could see glimpses of what was ahead for them. But I can't predict important things, like who's going to win an election. If I had that kind of sight, I'd spend my time down at the horse races betting on the ponies."

"Do you have any idea who's behind the harassment? If you can spot whoever's writing the symbols on your gate and throwing rocks through your window, maybe Ian can do something."

She looked horrified at my suggestion. "I don't want the police getting mixed up in my business. We live quietly and stay out of trouble, but the last thing we witches want is to get mixed up with the law. Trust me on this one."

"But it's Ian. You know he's our friend."

"He's a copper first. Besides, I'm still cross with him preferring that silly actress girl to you."

Violet might be kind of annoying, but she was certainly loyal.

"Okay, maybe we can take care of this ourselves. Have you got any idea who's been harassing you? I bet we could steer them gently in another direction using our magic."

She brightened up at that. "Lucy, that's the first time in weeks I've heard you voluntarily offer to do some magic. It's a great idea. I'm not positive, it was her, but I saw Elizabeth Palmer's best friend walking down my lane—shortly after that I discovered the symbols."

"You mean Nora?"

"Yes. The one I told would come into money. Where's the gratitude?"

Now wasn't that interesting. Nora, who kept turning up like a bad penny as Gran would say, was doing everything she could to push suspicion toward the witches. "I think it's time I paid a visit to Nora."

"Do I have to come?" It showed how much confidence Violet had lost that she didn't want to tag along.

"No. I'll drop you off at your cottage. Pack what you need for a few days. You're moving in with me."

I felt that she was about to argue, and then she said, "You're right. I will feel safer. And I'd rather live with you than my grandmother. Thanks."

I found the flimsiest of excuses to visit Nora. She had forgotten her receipt for the class last night.

Of course, I could just email it to her or give it to her next week, but I decided to deliver it in person. So at the end of the day, I drove yet again to Moreton-Under-Wychwood. Nora lived in a newer house in the outskirts. She wasn't in one of the darling stone cottages that make that whole area so picturesque but in a kind of subdivision of what they call new builds that all looked alike.

I found the address and pulled up in front of her house. I walked up the pathway that exactly split two sections of lawn edged all around by a flower bed. The home was neat and tidy and unremarkable. I walked up to the plain white front door and rang the doorbell. A dog began to bark like crazy from inside. I thought I might be out of luck and there was no one home when I heard footsteps approaching the door. I arranged my face into a pleasant expression as the door opened.

But it wasn't Nora standing there. It was her husband. I recognized him from the café. He was, like the house and the garden, neat, tidy, and unremarkable. He wore his medium-brown hair medium length, and it framed a pleasant face but one you would instantly lose in a crowd. His shoulders rounded inward as though he were protecting his heart.

He looked at me blankly. "Can I help you with something?"

I realized I was staring and dropped my gaze to the spaniel

that had stopped barking but was now making snuffling noises, clearly wanting to be noticed.

"My name is Lucy Swift. Your wife took a class from me last night and forgot her receipt, so I thought I'd drop it off."

I didn't give him the paper, hoping he would call his wife. He shook his head. "Nora's not here, I'm afraid." He sounded more sad than afraid. It was a Thursday night in Moreton-Under-Wychwood. Where on earth could she be?

I dropped to my knees and made friends with the dog. Nyx would not be pleased if she could see me consorting with the enemy, but luckily my familiar was in Oxford so I could be friends, temporarily, with a dog. "What a sweet pup," I gushed. "What's his name? Or her name?"

"This is Bessie." At her name, the dog's ears perked up, and she looked adoringly at her master.

I laughed. "Don't tell me, now she thinks she should get a treat?"

"You've obviously had dogs."

"No. But I've always loved them."

He didn't seem in any hurry to shut the door, and I was in no hurry to leave. "Will Nora be long? I could come back."

His face clouded. "She's over at our friend Jason's."

Still patting the dog, I glanced up. "Such a terrible tragedy. I was there that day, you know. I was helping in the fortune-telling booth."

"You were working for the witch?"

I tried not to jump to Violet's defense, knowing I'd get more out of him if I stayed friendly. Deliberately, I misunderstood him. "She's always been nice to me."

I continued, "I understand that you and your wife were very close to Elizabeth and Jason. I'm so sorry. It's been a terrible loss for you."

He laughed, but there was no humor in the sound. "No doubt you've heard the gossip. I imagine everyone has."

I could feel his pain. I noticed that as I worked more with my spell book and with my magic, I was increasingly sensitive to people's emotions. I felt such compassion for this poor man that I stood up and, looking right into his eyes, said, "Why didn't you go to visit Jason with Nora?"

He was obviously shocked that I had asked such a blunt, brutally honest question but, like someone who is desperate to talk and doesn't know where to turn, he said, "Why don't you come inside? I'll make you a cup of tea." He shrugged his shoulders. "If my loving wife isn't home by the time we finish our tea, you can leave the papers with me, and I'll see that she gets them."

I agreed, and he said, "I'm Tony, by the way."

$\mathcal{A}$s sad as I was for this betrayed husband, I was delighted to get inside Nora's house. Bessie was just as delighted to have me there and jumped up on my legs with both her front paws, letting me know that we were now fast friends. I leaned down and ruffled her head, making her long ears dance.

I followed Tony down the corridor that led to the kitchen. It was bare hardwood, and his slippers made a swishing sound as though he didn't pick his feet up when he walked. I followed, and my running shoes made no sound at all. Bessie was the noisy one, her paws clicking as she scampered beside me.

The kitchen was pretty much what I had expected. Clean and rather boring. I smelled chicken curry and saw the remains of a ready meal in the trash. There was only one meal, so presumably his wife had shared her dinner with Jason.

He put on the kettle and fussed about, getting a sugar pot out of the cupboard and a carton of milk from the fridge.

The newspaper was sitting beside a reclining chair in the den area off the kitchen, facing the TV, and I imagined that's where this poor man spent his lonely hours.

A large photograph of Nora and him on their wedding day dominated one wall of the den. A younger version of the sad man making tea gazed at his wife in that photograph, and you could see the adoration in his gaze. She, on the other hand, stared straight ahead at the camera as though unaware of her new husband.

There was a sideboard against one wall, and on its surface were more photographs. There was a picture of Nora, Tony, Elizabeth and Jason in the Caribbean. Another of Nora on her own, and then four of them on a skiing holiday. I walked over and studied the photographs. "I understand you're still going to go ahead with the anniversary cruise."

He jerked his head up as though we hadn't heard me correctly. "What?"

"That's what Nora said. That you're going ahead with the cruise and turning it into a memorial for Elizabeth. She said you were taking Elizabeth's ashes to bury her at sea."

He swore softly under his breath.

"Didn't you know?"

"Believe me, I'm always the last to know." The kettle boiled, and he poured hot water into the teapot. "I doubt I'll go, anyway." He glanced at me and back down to his task. "Fifth wheel and all that."

Had I understood him correctly? "Are you suggesting that you would stay home while your wife and Jason went on the cruise by themselves?"

He carried the tray over to the den area and put it down. Bessie got up and sniffed hopefully, and then, realizing there was nothing dog-oriented on that tray, she flopped down and put her head between her paws.

He said, "Even if the four of us had gone, Jason and Nora still would've been all by themselves on the cruise."

I felt his pain so acutely, I could hardly bear it. "How can you stand it? How can you stand to watch the woman you love carry on like that with your friend?"

He sat in his favorite chair. "Help yourself to tea."

I did. I poured myself a cup of tea and, without even asking, poured him one, too. Poor man. He looked like he could use a cup. "Milk and sugar?"

He nodded. "Thanks. One of each."

I made up his tea and stirred it and passed it over. Then I settled back with my own cup. I didn't particularly want tea, but I thought sharing this might lead to him sharing his troubles. I wanted to stretch out this visit and learn more about this peculiar foursome. Tony seemed like he was as eager to talk about his problems as I was to listen.

He sipped his tea and then finally answered my question. "I love Nora so much it's like a physical ache. I love her enough that I would rather see her happy than be happy myself."

I thought that was one of the saddest things I'd ever heard.

"It's not her fault, you see. She can't help herself. I think she loves Jason the way I love her. So I put up with it. So does Elizabeth." He winced. "*Did* Elizabeth. I can't believe she's gone."

He gazed over at the photograph of the four of them. "That was taken in Antigua. Our tenth wedding anniversary. At least when there were four of us, Liz and I had each other. It wasn't much, but we could commiserate."

"So Elizabeth knew?"

"Oh yes."

"Knew that her husband was having an affair with her best friend?"

He shook his head. "I wouldn't use the word affair. They were really more the couple than we were."

"Why didn't they ever, um, you know. Divorce you and marry each other?"

"Jason was so..." He hesitated, looking for the right word. "Meshed with Elizabeth's family. First, he worked in her family business. I think that house they lived in had belonged to her grandparents. He couldn't leave Elizabeth without leaving his whole livelihood. And Nora doesn't have any money. So we all put up with it."

"Including Elizabeth?" Sounded to me like she'd had more choices.

"It's hard to explain, but they weren't unhappy. None of us were. We're all basically nice people, and somehow we found a balance. Now, of course, that balance has shifted. The table only has three legs."

Tony shifted in his chair as though he'd sat on something sharp. "I imagine, now Jason is free, Nora will divorce me and marry him."

And then, in front of my horrified gaze, he began to weep.

I wanted to beg him not to cry. But I held my tongue because I sensed he needed the relief. Bessie got up off the floor, padded over and put her chin on his knee. He reached out blindly and patted his faithful dog. "You won't leave me, will you, old girl?"

She wagged her stubby tail.

I hesitated to intrude any further on his misery, but I was very curious about one thing. Did he know about the million-pound insurance policy?

Pretending to peruse the newspaper headlines, I waited until he'd got himself back under control. He apologized, but I was glad he'd let a little of his unhappiness out.

"Please, don't apologize. This is such a difficult time." I sipped more tea and then said, as though I'd just thought of it, "Did Elizabeth have life insurance, do you know?"

He was clearly startled by the question. "Why yes. They both did. So do Nora and I. It's common sense, isn't it? It's bad enough to lose your partner, but if you've got all the burden of the mortgage and bills, at least the insurance gives the bereaved partner a bit of breathing room."

I thought a million pounds would give a person a lot more than breathing room.

Like incentive.

～

VIOLET MOVED into my flat that night. When I got home from my visit to Nora's husband, my cousin was hauling an alarmingly large suitcase out of her car. I thought she might stay with me for a couple of days, but it looked as though she'd brought every scrap of clothing she owned. What had I done?

My face must have telegraphed my thoughts, for she laughed. "Oh, Lucy. If you could see your face. Don't worry, I'm not moving in permanently. I've brought a few magic supplies with me, and I thought we'd practice. You don't practice enough. As a more experienced witch, I can guide you."

Lucky me.

I helped her haul the beast of a suitcase up the stairs, and when we reached the living room, Nyx jumped down from the couch where she'd been sitting grooming herself and nosed around the case. Her tail began to twitch.

No doubt her sensitive familiar's nose picked up whatever magic ingredients were inside.

"I'm not sure we're going to have a lot of time to practice magic. I'm more interested in figuring out who killed Elizabeth, to get the pressure off you."

She rolled her gaze. "Multitasking, Lucy. It's called multitasking."

"When people talk about multitasking, they mean throwing on a load of laundry while you're checking email, or painting your nails while watching TV. I do not think solving a murder and practicing witchcraft counts as multitasking."

"Then we'll just have to combine the two. We'll use our magic powers to help solve this crime."

I'd never yet found that I could use magic for anything as useful as solving a crime. Still, the sooner we found out who killed Elizabeth, the sooner Violet could go back to her own home. I was a highly motivated sleuth. If magic would help, I was all over the magic.

While she unpacked in the guestroom, I multitasked by putting on the kettle for some chamomile tea while freshening Nyx's water and putting some fresh tuna in her dish. I was the master of efficiency.

When she came back into the kitchen dressed in bright pink cotton pajamas, she sat down at the kitchen table. I put the mug of chamomile in front of her and pushed the tin of cookies that Gran had baked that morning toward her. She opened it and made a sound like a squeak. "What is this?"

I leaned over and peeked in the tin. I was pretty surprised myself. "I must've run out of ginger again."

We both stared into the tin. Violet said, "Honestly, I thought your grandmother could only make ginger cookies."

"I guess she has the recipe for peanut butter cookies too."

She looked doubtful. "I don't know, Lucy. Things are getting strange around here."

I knew what she meant, but I was quite partial to peanut butter cookies. I took one and bit into it. It was perfect. Crunchy on the outside, slightly soft on the inside, bursting with peanut flavor.

Vi followed my lead and nodded her approval when she bit into her own cookie.

While we were sitting together, I related my conversation with Nora's husband. She didn't interrupt once, possibly because her mouth was constantly full. She seemed to have made her peace with Gran's wild culinary daring.

I didn't tell her Tony had cried because it seemed too personal and painful to share, but I did tell her that he now believed his wife would divorce him and marry Jason.

She swallowed, clearing her mouth enough to say, "He may think they're all very nice people, but with a million quid and his wife out of the way, Jason can now have everything he wants, including Nora."

I'd been thinking the same thing. "I think it's time I found another excuse to visit the grieving husband."

"Lucy? You can't go there alone. We just decided he probably killed his wife. You start snooping around, and he might kill you."

I didn't think he'd get rid of me in the middle of the day in a quiet village like Moreton-Under-Wychwood, but someone had got rid of his wife exactly that way. Violet said, "I'm coming with you."

I tried to look very bosslike. "And who is going to run Cardinal Woolsey's?"

She pouted. "That shop takes up a lot of our time."

I reached for a cookie. "It also pays us both a salary."

"There is that." She took one more cookie, put the lid back on the tin and resolutely pushed it toward me. "Keep those away from me."

I laughed and returned the tin to its usual place on the shelf so I wouldn't be tempted either.

I didn't think I had any reason to fear Jason, but I wasn't going to be foolish. I told Violet that I would ask Rafe to go with me.

"Excellent plan. If Jason Palmer causes you any trouble, Rafe will tear his throat out."

"And that should help us stay under the radar."

When I called Rafe the next morning, he said, "Lucy. I'm in the car now. I'm on my way to see you."

It was seriously creepy the way he so often turned up whenever I was thinking of him or needed him. "Why are you coming here?"

"Silversmith marks. I found something interesting."

I didn't have the heart to tell him our investigation seemed to be going in a different direction, so I thanked him and asked if he could drive me to Moreton-Under-Wychwood. "I want to talk to Jason Palmer in his home."

"He'd be at the dealership, surely?"

"No. I called there. There was a message saying they were closed today due to unforeseen circumstances."

"That's curious." He had a meeting later in the day, to assess a collection the Bodleian was thinking about purchasing, but until then he was at my disposal.

I dressed carefully, wanting to appear nonthreatening to a possible murderer, the kind of woman you open the door to. I chose a cheerful floral cotton dress, which I wore with sandals, as the day was once again warm. A blue cardigan that Theodore had knitted me went perfectly with my dress. Being an artist, he'd hand-painted large wooden buttons. Each was a tiny watercolor painting.

I kept my makeup simple and left my long blond hair to dry naturally. It was just easier that way.

I was ready to go when Violet rushed out of the guestroom, grabbed a cup of coffee and an apple out of the fruit bowl and headed down the stairs to the shop just as Rafe arrived. As her shoes hammered their way down the stairs, he shook his head. "That's quite remarkable, managing to be late for work when she's sleeping above the shop."

"Well, at least she's safe here."

For now.

CHAPTER 20

The Range Rover was deliciously cool with the air-conditioning on. Sitting behind the tinted windows, I felt like a celebrity.

As we drove, he said, "Remember the hallmarks you saw on the back of the watch Elizabeth Palmer bought at the white elephant sale?"

"Yes." It was hard to get too excited about that missing watch with so much evidence stacked against Jason Palmer.

"The stamped symbol DE was that of a watchmaker in Coventry. David Ealing's watches were unique. He made watches in the late nineteenth century, and every one had a special number in the movement. One of those watches was sold to one Jeremiah Timmins in 1890."

"Jeremiah Timmins? Was that—"

"Grayson's father, yes."

It was indeed interesting but probably irrelevant. I related my conversation with Nora's husband once more.

The car swerved and nearly went off the road as he turned to stare at me. "Are you completely mad?"

"Mad, like crazy? No. Speaking of crazy, get your eyes back on the road. What did I do?"

"Has it not occurred to you that Tony Betts is also a prime suspect in Elizabeth Palmer's murder?"

"What? Why?"

"He's besotted with his wife. He'd do anything for her." He let the words hang there. "Maybe he killed Elizabeth Palmer so his beloved wife could have the man she really wanted." His voice remained low, but the level of suppressed fury increased with every word. "And then you turn up on his doorstep asking a lot of nosy questions, all alone. Then, when he invited you into his house, where not a soul knew you were going, you followed him in. You could have been killed!"

Okay, when he put it like that, I could see I hadn't been very smart. But I was still alive, so that was something.

"But would Tony really kill Elizabeth just to make his wife happy? When that meant helping her leave him?"

He said, "I don't know. And neither do you." After a pause, he went on, "But no one had more reason to kill Elizabeth than Jason did. He gets a million pounds and all his troubles go away."

"Plus, now he's free to marry Nora Betts."

He shot me a glance full of disdain. "Murder as an act of love?"

"Yeah. I can't wait to see what Jason comes up with on Valentine's Day."

We drove through the High Street of the sleepy village. The house that had been Elizabeth's grandparents' and now, presumably, belonged to Jason was a little outside of town. It was a beautiful Victorian Gothic revival, with gargoyles and turrets. It was surrounded by neglected gardens that looked as though they needed a crew of landscapers to spruce them up. I guessed they hadn't wanted to waste money on gardening.

Rafe parked across the street, and just as we were about to

get out of the car, he put a restraining hand on my forearm. "Wait. What's our story?"

Oh, right. I hadn't got that far. "Let's go with a version of the truth. I called his car dealership, and it's closed today. I have a couple of questions about that car. Like whether I can get it in red." I sighed. "And if he'd like to lend me some of his million pounds so I can buy it."

I put my hand on the door latch, but once more he stopped me. "I think we're too late. Look."

I followed his gaze to a nondescript blue car, just slowing to turn into Jason Palmer's drive. Behind it followed a squad car. I was very glad that the windows were tinted. We watched as DI Thomas got out of the first car with another man in a similar suit.

Two uniformed officers climbed out of the second car and, after a brief conference on the pavement, the two detectives headed up the path toward the house. One of the uniforms remained by the road, and the other ran around the outside of the house, presumably looking for a back door in case Jason tried to run.

"It seems the police have come to the same conclusion you have."

I looked at him curiously. "You don't agree?"

"Oh, he's clearly the person with the most to gain. I just wonder how someone who was ruthless enough to kill his wife wasn't ruthless enough to make a go of a car dealership, that's all."

"Maybe it wasn't ruthlessness, but panic, that drove him to kill his wife."

"Perhaps."

Rafe and I watched until the two detectives emerged with Jason. The two uniformed cops walked behind, and one of them was carrying a bow and arrow. Jason Palmer wore the stunned look of a man who has just been arrested. I'd have hazarded a guess that it was the first time. Jason didn't look like a hardened criminal. He looked like a boy caught out in mischief.

Rafe waited until the two police cars had driven away. He looked over at me. "Do you want to take a look inside?"

I felt my forehead crease in puzzlement. "You mean break into that man's house?"

"Yes."

"What for? They found his bow and arrow, and they've got Jason. What do we want inside their house?"

He shook his head. "I don't know. I feel like we're missing something."

I didn't want to break into Jason's house. That seemed like yet another blow to a man who'd suffered plenty. So I told Rafe I really needed to get back to the shop and check on Violet.

He didn't argue with me, just pulled smoothly out into the road.

WALKING BACK into Cardinal Woolsey's felt like slipping my arms into a well-worn and long-loved sweater, the kind you snuggle down in and watch TV when no one is coming over.

It had grown on me, my little knitting shop in Oxford. From an unwanted burden, the shop now seemed like a place of warmth and comfort and, I supposed, safety. Not everyone would feel safe with a nest of vampires living beneath them, but I sure did.

Rafe dropped me at the door and said he had a few things to do before his meeting at the Bodleian.

Violet was alone, sitting behind the cash desk chatting on her phone. She glanced up and looked a bit guilty when she saw me and hastily said she had to go. She dropped her phone back in her purse, saying, "It's been a really quiet morning."

Pointedly, I began to tidy the shelves. Guiltily, she grabbed the duster. Nyx jumped down from her usual spot in the window, strolled over and rubbed up against my legs, circling me until with a laugh I gave in and picked her up. She purred loudly, letting me know she'd missed me. "I missed you, too," I said, putting my cheek against her sleek, black head.

She then crawled up and over my shoulder to hang there, heavy, warm and comforting, leaving me with two hands free to continue tidying the shelves and the rumble of contented cat in my ears.

We remained like that for about fifteen minutes, then all of a sudden Nyx went rigid, stopped purring and let out a low, warning growl. I turned to the door to see a woman fling open the shop door and burst in, so much anger sparking off her it was like a walking fireworks display.

I recognized her at once. "Nora. What's wrong?"

She ignored me and pointed a shaking finger at Violet. "You!"

Violet backed up until she hit the wall of cashmere yarns. She looked at me, beseeching.

I put Nyx down on the floor and walked forward. "Nora," I said quite firmly. Since we were in my shop, I wasn't going to let her intimidate my assistant. "What's wrong? Is it your knitting?"

Though, from her fury, I doubted it was a knitting issue. She swung around to me, and I saw so much rage on her face, it crossed my mind that this was a woman who was capable of murder. "Your little assistant here is a witch. She killed Elizabeth, and now she's letting my poor Jase take the blame. He's been arrested!" *Jase?* Seriously?

She turned back to Violet, who hadn't moved and looked as though she might spend the rest of her life with her back against the cashmere. "You'd better go to the police and tell them that you did it, or you'll be sorry."

I had planned to be appeasing, but at those words, I felt my own anger rise. I was a witch, too. Besides, Violet was my cousin, and nobody spoke to her that way, not on my turf.

They do say the best defense is a good offense. I crossed my arms and stalked toward her. "Maybe you should go to the police and admit that you've been vandalizing Violet's property and harassing her. What you're doing is illegal."

She looked as though I had slapped her. And then she laughed, a very humorless laugh. "She must've put a spell on you. Didn't you hear me? Your assistant is a witch."

I moved my hands to my hips. "There's a word that rhymes with witch, and that is what you're being right now."

She drew in her breath on a sharp gasp. "How dare you?" I felt anger crackling from me, Nyx and Violet. My fingertips were getting hot. If I wasn't careful, I'd ignite.

A male voice intruded. "Lucy? Is everything all right?"

Ian Chisholm stepped in. I didn't think I'd ever been so happy to see him. "Why, Detective Inspector Chisholm." I enunciated the words very clearly for Nora's benefit.

Ian looked slightly startled that I was referring to him by his official title, but a quick glance at our tense trio must've clued him in.

He said, "My auntie's asked me to pick her up some wool. But I can wait, if you're busy."

He hadn't suggested coming back, for which I was grateful. Nora glared at both of us and said, "This isn't over." And then she swept out.

Violet slumped into the chair behind the cash desk as though her legs wouldn't hold her up anymore. "I'm so sick of this. I'm going to have to move."

Ian asked, "What's going on? That woman's from Moreton-Under-Wychwood, isn't she?"

I nodded, feeling a little shaken myself. I glanced at Violet, but she shook her head slightly. She did not want to get into the witch thing with Ian. I didn't, either. Hopefully Nora would think better of going to the police with her crazy notion that witches had killed her friend.

Hopefully.

"She had a complaint about the knitting lessons I'm running there."

I didn't think he believed me, but since two pairs of witch eyes were currently focused on him, he let it go.

THE SECOND KNITTING lesson we ran in Moreton-Under-Wychwood was even better attended than the first one. The woman who'd blamed Violet when both her online dates had canceled on her showed up. She came up to my table and sighed. "Since it looks like I'll be single for some time, I might as well take up knitting." Her hair looked as though she'd styled it with a lawn mower, and she had what looked like dribbled egg yolk down the front of her shirt. "I should get a cat, too, for company."

Since I'd recently taken up knitting and now had a cat, I treated her comments as though they were meant to be funny. *Hahaha.*

I still had a few kits left, and Sylvia was perfectly happy to take in some new students. She obviously thought word had spread about what a great teacher she was, and perhaps it had, but I suspected Jason's arrest for murder had a lot to do with it. Here, anyone in the community who wanted to could sit in a circle, knitting and gossiping.

And it was certainly juicy gossip. To my surprise, Nora showed up. Instead of apologizing for her dreadful behavior in my shop, she glanced around pointedly. "That witch isn't here, is she?"

"No." I didn't bother telling her she was being taught to knit by vampires.

Her eyes were swollen and red, but I didn't have much

150

sympathy for her, knowing how unhappy she and *Jase* had made her own husband.

News had spread faster than a flu bug that Jason had been about to lose his business and home and that his wife had carried life insurance worth a million pounds.

A woman with a rather penetrating voice was currently regaling everyone with the details, though it was clear everyone present already knew. Her knitting needles rattled away at the same rate as her conversation.

Her neighbor said, "But surely there are better ways to do away with a spouse than a bow and arrow. It's so brutal, and he could easily have wounded her instead of killing her."

Rapidly, the first speaker counted her row of stitches before replying. "If my Bert had lost all our money, I'd bash his head in with a frying pan. I suppose that's rather brutal, isn't it?"

Nora had been listening to the woman chattering away in gathering wrath and suddenly strode forward into the group. Instant, awkward silence fell over everyone, and half the needles stop moving. The other half kept going so the clicking sounded like the needles had carried on gossiping without us. She glared at the woman who'd just threatened to bash her husband over the head. "Jason didn't kill Elizabeth. He'd never kill her." She turned a slow circle to take in every person in the knitting circle. "He'd never hurt anyone."

CHAPTER 21

*N*ora looked quite wild. Her hair was a mess of tangles, her eyes wide and underlined with dark circles, and the bottoms of her jeans were crusty with dried mud. She glanced around. "I came here today to get some help from all of you. You're supposed to be our friends. Jason's a good man. How many of you have bought your cars from him? Enjoyed the excellent service that he gives?"

This didn't elicit an immediate response, and finally one of the women said, "But selling cars is his business. I never heard that he gave us any discounts or treated us special in any way because we were his neighbors."

She tried another tack. "What about all the things he's done for this community? How many of your children has he coached?"

"He coached my son and daughter in archery."

There was deathly silence. I thought we were all picturing poor Elizabeth dead, an arrow sticking out of her chest.

"Just because a man is a good archer doesn't mean he's a killer."

Very gently, Hilary Beaumont said, "But it doesn't look very good when his wife is killed with an arrow. We all know that Jason is an expert archer." She looked at Nora with kindness but also a hint of steel. "I'm very sorry for you, Nora, but you must see the evidence against him is quite damning. His financial situation was precarious. He was close to losing everything, and Elizabeth's death conveniently wipes out all his debts."

"But he loved Elizabeth."

Hilary Beaumont put her knitting aside. "But she wasn't the only woman he loved, was she, Nora?"

Nora threw up her hands. "I can't believe you people. I can't stand and listen to this. You go back to your gossiping and backstabbing. I know he didn't do it, and I'm going to prove it."

She turned and began heading for the door, and her face was such a picture of tragedy that I felt some reluctant sympathy for her even though I thought that she and Jason had made their respective spouses very unhappy.

"Wait."

At the commanding tone, Nora turned. It was Joanna who had put down her knitting and stood up. She walked over and put an arm around Nora's shoulders, drawing her back to the group. "Nora's right. Jason's been our neighbor and our friend and a pillar of our community for twenty-five years. He and Elizabeth were planning a cruise for their silver wedding anniversary. The police evidence is only circumstantial. Lots of people get into financial trouble and don't kill their spouses. I love Moreton-Under-Wychwood. I love this community, how safe it feels, and how much we all care about each other. Maybe it's time for us to reach out and help one of our neighbors who is in trouble."

Around the circle, women glanced at one another, gauging what the other knitters were thinking.

The woman who'd threatened to bash her own husband over the head if he ever lost her money paused with her knitting in her lap. "Well, what do you want us to do?"

Joanna seemed at a loss.

Sylvia looked significantly at me. I supposed I had the most experience of murder of anyone in this room, unfortunately. I stood up. "The police believe Jason murdered his wife because he had the means and the motive. But no one saw him do it. The best way to prove he didn't kill Elizabeth is to find out what exactly he was doing at the moment she died."

I came out from behind my table and went to stand on the other side of Joanna. "Did anyone see Jason around the time that the murder took place?"

Dierdre Gunn said, "I think I saw him earlier that day, but who keeps track of time at a village fête?"

I thought if anyone had kept track of Jason's movements, it would've been Nora. "Nora? Do you know where he was at that time?"

She bit her lip and looked miserable. Also guilty. "He was home, packing." She looked down at the floor, and her previously pale countenance took on a ruddy hue. "We were going on a golf trip."

"Do you have any proof that he was actually there?"

Her head came up with that, and she glared at me. "I've already told you, Jason's a good man. If he told me he was at home packing, then that's where he was."

Of course she wasn't helping his case at all. Merely underlining the fact that Jason had been a poor husband and likely an adulterous one too.

Hilary said, "From Jason and Elizabeth's house to the village hall, where the arrow was shot from, is an easy walk. He could have slipped down the back lane and got into the hall. No one would have seen him. We were all at the fair."

Nora made a sound like a shriek. "You're supposed to be helping me prove that he didn't do it, not tightening the noose around his neck."

She shook her head. "I'm sorry for you, Nora. I really am.

But Joanna said it herself. We are a close-knit community, and we all love that we feel safe here. I'm sorry, but if Jason did this terrible thing, then he needs to go to jail. Not only to pay for Elizabeth's death, but so the rest of us can sleep at night."

"But he didn't do it, I tell you, he didn't. He couldn't."

There was a terrible silence, and then Joanna spoke again. "Here's what I think we should do. Every one of us must go home and ask everybody in our household—that's husbands, children, elderly parents who didn't get out to the fête—did anyone see Jason? Did they see him pottering around in the garden? Perhaps he was carrying golf clubs out to his car?"

Nora nodded, eagerly. "If we can prove that he was at home during that crucial few minutes, then we can prove that he's innocent." She looked around. "A man cannot be in two places at once."

Those words rattled in my head and echoed. Where had I heard them before? I remembered then that the former police officer, Harry Bloom, had said the very same thing about the cold-case murder.

While everyone was gathered here and already tasked with trying to prove Jason innocent, I said, "I understand a man was murdered here thirty years ago and that case was never solved."

The woman who'd been gossiping so loudly when Nora came in nodded her head vigorously. "Yes. Grayson Timmins. It was a dreadful thing. I was frightened for weeks. We all were. He was bludgeoned to death by someone who was trying to steal his valuables."

I said, "I'm sure it was investigated thoroughly at the time, but those of you who were here then, did you see any strangers in the village that day?"

"That's what was so peculiar about it. No one could recall seeing anyone in the neighborhood who shouldn't have been." She chuckled, and I thought she was half laughing at herself.

"And believe me, Lucy, in this village, everyone knows everyone else's business."

"Can anyone think of any reason why these two murders might be related?"

From the way they were glancing amongst themselves, I knew people had been debating this topic already in private.

Nora said, "But Jason wasn't even here then."

"Exactly," I said. I didn't like Jason much, but if he was innocent, he shouldn't go to jail. No one said anything, and so I continued, "If we could find a connection between Grayson Timmins and Elizabeth Palmer, maybe we'd be able to find out if the same person killed them both."

Dierdre Gunn picked up her knitting again and stabbed the needles through her ball of wool before pushing the whole thing into her knitting bag. "Those witches were here thirty years ago. Maybe Jason didn't do it. Maybe it was witchcraft."

Oh, this was not going in the direction I wanted it to. I was about to argue when fortunately Joanna spoke up. "I don't think the police are going to be interested in our theories about witchcraft."

Joanna nodded in my direction. "Lucy thought up an excellent idea. Let's work together to help Jason." As the gossipy woman was about to argue with her, she put up her hand. "If he's guilty, I'm the first one to believe he should be punished. But I believe, as Nora does, that Jason isn't a killer. Let's help our neighbor. If he's innocent, let's prove it. We'll all go home and talk to our loved ones tonight. Let's reconvene here on Friday. Is that convenient?"

Everyone nodded.

She glanced at me and Clara and Sylvia. "And would you three be available to come back? You seem like an integral part of our knitting circle now."

We were certainly an integral part of the sleuthing circle,

and I for one wanted to make sure the right people were punished.

I glanced at Sylvia, and she nodded, such a slight up and down of her chin that I knew she really didn't want to come back, and I thought I understood why.

If a community was going to go all hysterical about a few witches in their midst, what would they do if they discovered they were being taught knitting by vampires?

WHEN THE VAMPIRES and I had wedged ourselves back into Gran's car, and I'd managed to navigate to the route that led me back to Oxford, I asked the other two for their thoughts.

Sylvia had been more engaged in teaching knitting, but Clara had had a perfect opportunity to observe quietly. However, Clara always deferred to Sylvia, and so she let the glamorous former actress speak first. Sylvia said, "Frankly, I find this whole affair quite puzzling. We've got a dead woman whose husband had all the reasons in the world to do away with her, so it seems as though the police must've arrested the correct person. I feel that bringing in this cold case from decades ago is simply muddying the waters."

"Clara?" I asked.

Clara always liked to think the best of people, which could be surprisingly helpful. She didn't disappoint me now. "It was nice of Joanna to support poor Nora. The woman is clearly distraught."

Sylvia asked, "But is she distraught because she's beginning to suspect that the man she loves is a murderer?"

I thought that was a really good point. And this was where Clara being so nice about everyone paid off. She said, "But Nora wasn't the only one who believed in his innocence. These people have lived with each other for such a long time, and they all know Jason and knew Elizabeth. I felt there was quite a bit of support for him. Of course, ladies always gossip over their knitting, but I didn't sense any fear when Jason's name came up. And you'd expect people to be frightened, wouldn't you? If they'd been living with a murderer?"

"Clara, what did you think about the way they reacted to the idea of linking that cold case with Elizabeth's murder?"

"Well, it's an interesting possibility, isn't it? It would narrow down the field to people who had known Grayson Timmins and would have been both old enough to murder him thirty years ago, and yet, still young enough to shoot a deadly arrow. In mortal years that would suggest that they must've been at least teenagers thirty years ago and no older than about seventy now."

Sylvia shook her silver head. "I for one do not think the cases are linked. That woman who wants to prove her boyfriend is innocent is clutching at that idea the way a drowning person keeps clutching at any bit of flotsam and jetsam."

"If there is a link," I said, "it's that watch."

Sylvia said, "You put a lot of stock into that watch. But don't forget, my dear, you only saw it briefly. Then you had the shock of finding that woman murdered, and quite a bit of time elapsed before you saw that picture of Grayson Timmins. And it wasn't even a photograph of the watch, it was a painting. Painters notoriously take liberties."

I knew that Sylvia was right and it was quite possible that either my eyes or my memory was playing tricks on me. And yet, it was peculiar to have two murders of people who seemed to be unlikely victims in a relatively short period of time.

"Sylvia," I said. "You're right. I believe that watch links the two murders, but I'm relying on pretty flimsy evidence." The last thing I wanted was for Jason Palmer to get away with murdering his wife and be rewarded with a fortune all because

I had put together a link between the two murders that was tenuous at best. However, I didn't want an innocent man to suffer for a crime he hadn't committed while the true murderer got away with not one but two murders.

"I know what I have to do. I can't believe I didn't think of it before. Harry Bloom. He's a retired police detective who moved to Moreton-Under-Wychwood. He was one of the detectives on the Grayson Timmins case, and he was at the fête."

"Now you're thinking like a sleuth, Lucy. Well done." Sylvia didn't toss out praise like it was Halloween candy, so I took a moment to drink in the compliment.

She continued, "The life insurance company won't thank you for proving Jason Palmer didn't kill his wife."

"Why?" I took my eyes off the road to glance at her.

"Because if he's convicted of murdering his wife, the insurer won't have to pay out the life insurance."

"Poor Jason. A lot of people seem keen to convict him and not always for the purest of reasons."

"It's human nature. We don't like to think of killers in our midst, so we try to convict killers as quickly as possible so that people can feel safe and comfortable again."

I knew she was right. And since my cousin Violet had been pulled into this mess, and dragged me into it by becoming my temporary roommate, I was one of those looking forward to this case being solved so that I could sleep better at night.

CHAPTER 22

The cottage where Harry and Emily Bloom had retired looked idyllic. Made of stone and surrounded by pretty gardens, it looked like something out of a fairy tale: the roses climbing up the side of the house, the profusion of flowers and even a wishing well surrounded by bright, blooming poppies.

I wondered if, after a career spent dealing with criminals and the aftermath of crime, whether Harry Bloom had been drawn particularly by the fairy-tale aspect of this cottage. Or perhaps his wife had wanted it. I walked up the winding stone path to the front door but detoured when I saw a man in a straw hat bent over a flower bed with a trowel in his hand. I headed around the side of the house toward him, and sure enough, it was Harry Bloom himself.

I wasn't sure what kind of reception I'd receive, but I went with a cheerful and confident, "Hello, there."

He turned, and I watched him go through the effort of first recognizing me and then remembering where he'd met me. I saw the moment he placed me. He brushed his hands on his knees and rose to his feet. "Hello. You're the young lady from the fortune-telling booth."

"Yes. I was very sorry to hear about your mother-in-law." Violet had again been correct. However, thanks to her uncanny fortune-telling abilities, Mrs. Bloom had been able to help her mother during her illness. I hoped it would make the Blooms charitably inclined to Violet and to me.

"Thank you. My wife stayed on in Yorkshire, to help with the grandchildren and to sort out the house and things."

I merely nodded.

"I thought I'd better come back in case I was needed. I heard the police reopened the investigation into the Timmins case."

Both our gazes traveled to the flower bed he was currently working on, and he made a face. "Seems I was wrong about being needed."

I wanted his help, but I had to tread carefully. I didn't know how much he was at liberty to discuss the details of an old case. I began by saying, "That fortune-teller is my cousin Violet. She's having a hard time right now, people in the village are blaming her for Elizabeth Palmer's death."

He nodded, not looking a bit surprised. "I heard something about witchcraft at the pub." A series of empty flowerpots from the nursery sat beside half a dozen full ones. He'd been planting petunias, and the bright trumpets of red, pink, purple, and white were like bursts of light in a dark room. "As you know, I don't believe in all that nonsense, but she did have an uncanny knack of getting the future right."

Oh great. If this rational man joined the witch hunters, there was no hope for any of us.

"I'm glad your wife was able to see her mother before it was too late."

"Yes. So were we. She'd have been gutted not to be there."

He looked at his nearly finished planting once more and then said, "Can I make you a cup of tea?"

I appreciated his politeness, but I could tell that he really wanted to finish his planting. "Why don't I help you finish? And then perhaps we can have tea."

"Brilliant. I admit I'd like to get them in the ground so they don't dry out. I thought they'd be a nice surprise when my wife comes home."

I liked this man and, fortunately, I was wearing jeans and a T-shirt. I happily dropped to my knees in the grass. I eased plants out of their little plastic pots. They were packed six to a pot, and so I separated them as I could see he had done and handed them to him one by one for planting. It was pleasant under the sun. Bees buzzed around us, clearly waiting for us to finish so they could give in to the lure of those bright blooms. Birds swooped and played, and a fat squirrel paused to watch us for a minute before going back about his business.

I felt guilty about my own garden. The only reason it hadn't completely gone to seed was that Gran toiled regularly in the middle of the night to prune and weed. I really needed to step up and do more.

It didn't take very long to finish the planting, and then Harry Bloom got me to water the newly planted petunias while he tidied up the pots and put the garden tools away. When we were finished, he nodded with satisfaction.

"Right. I'll put the kettle on. I think we've earned a nice cuppa."

We had tea in a gazebo in their back garden. He settled back contentedly. "I do love it here, you know. There are badgers who come nearly every night, and the odd deer."

"It's beautiful."

He leaned forward as though about to impart a great secret. "And I'm bored witless."

This was the perfect opening for what I wanted to talk to

him about. "I remember when we first met, you told me you had investigated a murder here."

His eyes crinkled in a smile, but they were wary too. "And I recall telling you that you'd be a very good addition to a police force."

"I don't want to work for the police, but I am interested in proving that Violet had nothing to do with Elizabeth Palmer's death."

"But the police have arrested her husband."

"I'm not sure everyone in the village believes he killed his wife."

He still looked wary. "I was surprised to find a fear of witches here."

He should have been in the coffee shop when we were nearly mobbed.

"But surely she's not a suspect. Wasn't she inside her tent giving a reading at the very moment that woman was killed?"

"People seem to think she may have cast a spell on that woman and somehow killed her."

He shook his head. "Superstitious nonsense. What can I do to help?"

"Do you think there could be any connection between Grayson Timmins's murder thirty years ago and the one that just occurred?"

He rubbed his thumb along the edge of the table as though the answers might be written there in braille. I noticed a rim of dirt around the edge of his fingernail where he hadn't quite managed to scrub all the evidence of his gardening activities away. "It's funny, a young detective from Oxford asked me that very question. DI Chisholm."

The way he looked at me prompted me to say, "I know DI Chisholm."

"It's interesting. He asked me if you'd been to see me yet. You seem to have a bit of a reputation as an amateur sleuth."

I shook my head. "Not by choice, I assure you."

"Some people have a gift. Perhaps nosing out crime is yours?"

I had other gifts, and I had no intention of telling him about them. He didn't believe in our kind, anyway. Or so he said.

"I just want to take the heat off Violet. You see, she's staying in my spare room until people stop throwing rocks at her house."

His relaxed pose was gone in an instant. He straightened up, and his eyes went from lazily amused to sharp and businesslike. "She should report that to the police. Does she have any idea who's behind it?"

"No. She didn't see them." However, after the way people had acted in the coffee shop, I thought there were a lot of possible suspects.

"I'll tell you what I can. It's been thirty years, so I may be fuzzy on a few details. I've thought about that case often over time, though. For some reason it stayed with me."

"Tell me what happened."

He settled back in his chair once more. "I was called in to the crime scene, but I wasn't first to arrive. That's a pity. It's good to see people and watch reactions during moments of acute stress. They often give away more than they intend to or tell secrets that they normally hold tight. However, by the time I arrived, uniforms were already on the scene. The boy called it in. He was the one who found the body."

"When you say 'the boy,' do you mean Robert Beasley?" I thought how awful it would have been for him to discover his father like that. I recalled the terrible aura hanging around the dining room. The echo of trauma was still there.

"That's right. He said he arrived home to find his stepfather dead. His mother had been out at her evening class. She was taking French. She went every Thursday. When she arrived home, her son took her straight into the library, and he handled everything. She was quite content not to see her husband's body."

"She didn't even check that her husband was dead? Is that normal behavior?"

"There is no such thing as normal in a murder case. But certainly many people would prefer not to see their loved one like that."

"But Robert Beasley must have been a teenager." I recalled the dreamy man who was late for everything. I couldn't imagine entrusting something so important to him.

"He was seventeen. As cool as a cucumber, in fact. Was it shock? Possibly. Or a well-prepared act."

"But why would Robert Beasley want to kill his father?"

"You must remember, first of all, that Grayson Timmins wasn't his father."

"Right. The way he talks about him, he seems like he was very fond of him and thought of him as a father."

His eyes narrowed on my face. "Where did you get that idea from?"

"I've met both Mr. and Mrs. Beasley. I bought a poodle lamp from the white elephant, and I had to go to their house to pick it up."

His eyes widened, and for a man accustomed to hearing murderers' confessions, I suspected it took a great deal to shock him. "You bought that poodle lamp?"

I couldn't be bothered to give him my story about how cute and kitschy it was. "All right. I wanted to get inside that house and talk to them both. The lamp was the only thing I could remember being at the white elephant sale."

"And you could be fairly certain it wouldn't have sold."

"Mrs. Beasley mentioned how the house is essentially unchanged from when Robert Beasley's parents lived there. And then I met the man himself. He mentioned his happy boyhood."

"That's one of the things that bothered me from the beginning. That happy childhood theory is unsupported by village gossip."

That was interesting. "You think he lied?"

"From what I learned about Grayson Timmins, he was a rigid authoritarian. He believed in a hard work ethic and no imagination. The boy was a middling student at best and a dreamer. He wasn't a bad athlete, but not good enough to excel in that or anything."

"But we all know how notoriously village gossip can be wrong."

"If Timmins was so fond of that boy, why didn't he adopt him?"

"That's right. He didn't have the same last name."

"When I asked Mrs. Timmins the question, she said her ex-husband wouldn't allow it. But it turned out they hadn't seen the ex-husband in years. Consensus in the village was that Timmins refused to bestow his name on someone who didn't live up to it."

That sentiment accorded with the impression I'd had from the man in that painting.

"So you think Robert Beasley lied about his happy childhood?"

"I do."

I looked him directly in the eye. "Do you also believe that Robert Beasley killed Grayson Timmins?"

He held my gaze but didn't answer right away. "I had no proof. The boy claimed he'd been at running practice after school. He came home and found his father dead."

"Running practice. Round a track?"

He nodded, approving. "Cross country. They ran for an hour. He'd have had to be super-humanly quick to get from the school grounds back here, kill Timmins, stage the robbery, clean himself up and get rid of any evidence that connected him to the crime." He tapped his fingers on the tabletop. "But yes. I'm convinced he did it. I think Timmins berated him constantly and one day he snapped."

"Do you think he could have killed Elizabeth?"

"Of course he could have. But why?"

"I have an idea about that. First, tell me what was stolen."

"Allegedly stolen. Not one item ever showed up. Usually, burglars fence the valuables and they turn up here and there. But none of the supposedly stolen items ever came to light."

"What was allegedly taken?"

"Grayson Timmins was killed with a sterling candlestick. A very large, heavy, ornate one. It had a mate, and that disappeared. So did a Georgian tea set. Timmins had a valuable coin collection. That was gone as well."

"Where was the coin collection kept?"

He nodded. "Excellent question. It was kept upstairs in Timmins's bedroom. This was separate from his wife's. Interestingly, nothing was taken from her, and she had some very nice jewelry. And Grayson Timmins's silver pocket watch was gone. It was the item everyone most remembered about him."

"Okay," I said. "Maybe this is crazy, but I have a theory."

He looked at me. "And I have nothing but time."

"On the day that Elizabeth Palmer was killed, she was very excited because she had bought her husband a watch for his silver anniversary gift."

His eyes sharpened on my face. "What kind of watch?"

I smiled at him and repeated the words he'd recently said to me. "That's exactly the right question. It was a pocket watch. Sterling silver. She showed me the hallmarks the way you do when you're excited about something. She got it from the white elephant sale. I didn't think too much about it, though it did look like a very nice watch if you like antique pocket watches. What was curious was that after she was killed, the watch disappeared."

"What? Are you sure?"

Now I wasn't so sure. "I think so."

"Has anyone checked with the police to see if it was among her personal effects?"

I couldn't tell him I had a vampire network with excellent connections in the police, so I gave him an open-ended question. "If they had found an antique pocket watch by her body, wouldn't we have heard about it by now?"

"Tell me more about this watch. I could make a call or two. I may not be an active detective anymore, but I still have connections."

"I think I might recognize that watch if I saw a picture of it." I held my gaze steady on his. I could see him debating with himself. Finally, he shrugged. "I made two copies of everything in that file, and I never gave them back. Technically I shouldn't be sharing them with you, but you're not a suspect in any way. What are they going to do? Fire me?"

I tried not to look too eager, but I was beyond thrilled. As though he'd made a momentous decision, he gathered up the tea things and said, "Follow me."

I did. We went in through the back door that led directly into a kitchen. It seemed a happy, inviting place, painted cheerful yellow. One wall contained an open stone hearth.

Even though his wife wasn't home, Harry Bloom kept the place neat and tidy. Much neater and tidier than I kept my home, I realized with a pang of shame.

After placing the tea things onto the kitchen counter, he led the way through a living room so cozy I could imagine curling up with a good book. I could see which chair was Mrs. Bloom's, as a basket of wool sat beside it containing a partly finished sweater. It was blue and decorated with trucks, no doubt for a grandson.

We continued up a flight of stairs and into a home office. There were neat shelves containing stamp catalogues and books about stamp collecting. When I commented on his hobby, he said, "It's important to have activities when you retire."

He turned to a filing cabinet against the wall. The drawer opened fluidly, and it took him no time at all to find the file he wanted. I got the feeling he'd consulted it fairly recently.

He placed the folder on his desk, turned on a desk lamp and flipped past what looked to be written statements and reports to a collection of photocopies. They weren't as sharp as the original photographs would have been but definitely better than nothing.

He said, "These photographs had been taken for insurance purposes, so the details were quite good."

I looked carefully at the pictures of the watch, front, back and open.

"I'm almost certain this is the watch Elizabeth Palmer bought for her husband." I pointed to the vine design on the front as well as the hallmarks on the back.

"I thought I recognized it from the painting of Grayson Timmins hanging in the Beasleys' dining room, but seeing the photo of the hallmarks on the back makes me nearly certain."

"What kind of fool puts the very evidence that confirms him a murderer into a white elephant sale?"

"Mrs. Beasley was in charge of the white elephant. She told me she'd rooted around in her own house to add some items to the sale and that her husband wasn't too pleased."

He looked up at his boxes of stamps. "It's exactly the kind of thing my wife would do. She'd see a box of old stamps and think they had no value. She's always trying to get me to pare down my collection."

He turned off the light. "Well, I now have an even stronger sense that Robert Beasley killed his father. He'd always kept it hidden, and his wife found it and put it in the white elephant sale."

I nodded. "And Robert Beasley saw Elizabeth Palmer at the fair with that watch that would prove him to be the murderer. He had no option but to kill her, or so he thought. Having got away with murder once, perhaps he thought he could do it again?"

"It's a fine theory, Lucy. What we're missing is proof."

$\mathcal{I}$ knew that both Harry Bloom and all the other police officers who had worked on the murder case all those years must have gone over and over Robert Beasley's alibi.

"Timelines," I said. "Everything seems to revolve around time. Grayson Timmins was obsessively punctual, while Robert Beasley takes tardiness to a whole new level. He's a mass of contradictions. He says his childhood was happy, but no one else thinks so. He seems slow and dreamy, but his hobby's running."

"He had a second sport."

Something about the way Harry Bloom threw out that piece of information made my stomach jump.

"He was on the school archery team."

I FELT FRUSTRATED AND WISHED, not for the first time, that I'd spent more time becoming a better witch. Someone who could see through lies and find the truth.

I stood up and thanked Harry Bloom for his help. I knew I sounded disappointed, and so did he when he said, "I'm worried that the wrong man is going to be convicted of this murder."

I nodded. "And the right man is going to get away with it yet again."

He banged his fist into the palm of his hand. "Unless we can draw a connection between Robert Beasley's stepfather and Elizabeth Palmer."

He'd been a cop for more than three decades, while I had only been an amateur sleuth for less than half a year. "How do we do that?"

The retired police detective with decades of experience under his belt slumped back in his chair. "I have no idea."

I walked back to his desk and gazed into that open file. As I did, my fingers began to tingle ever so slightly. Normally that happened when my anger got out of control, but I'd become so much better at keeping my emotions in check that I was rarely embarrassed by electric sparks shooting out of the ends of my fingers. I glanced down in horror, but my hands looked perfectly normal. Some people had a nose for trouble. I wondered if I had fingertips of intuition.

In case that was it, I asked if I could look over the folder one more time. I looked at each of the photographs again. What was I missing? Was there a clue here somewhere?

I flipped over the pages. There was a photograph of quite an old land deed. I said, "What's this?"

Harry Bloom looked over my shoulder. "One of the leads I followed that didn't go anywhere. The murdered man's ancestors owned a great deal of the land in and surrounding the village. Of course, what hadn't already been sold off came to the wife and, when she died, to her son."

I was staring at one area of the map. My fingers were really tingling now. "This area wasn't developed thirty years ago. But that's where Nora and her husband live, in a subdivision that can't be more than ten or twenty years old."

And then my brow wrinkled in puzzlement. "This shaded area, was all this land owned by Beasley's father?"

"Yes. Anything built on it was leasehold."

"But this plot here, unless I'm reading this map wrong, is where Elizabeth lived." I felt very confused. "But I've been there. It's a Victorian manor house."

"That's right. But the land beneath it belonged to Grayson Timmins at the time of his death and was passed on to his son."

This was very confusing to an American. "You mean, you can buy a house in England and not own the land?"

"Yes. People often own houses but not the land they're built on. They pay yearly land rent, and there's a set of covenants attached to the lease. They may need the permission of the leaseholder to do things like dig up hedges, extend the house or add buildings to the land."

I looked at the map. At one time, most of the village must've paid rent to Grayson Timmins.

"We know that Jason Palmer was in financial trouble. Maybe he and his wife stopped paying the rent?" But who shot someone in the heart with an arrow because they hadn't paid their rent on time? It didn't make sense.

He was staring down at the old map as intently as I was. "No. It doesn't make sense. But it's the first time we've found a connection." He tapped his fingertips on the edge of that paper. "Well done, Lucy. It would be well worth finding out what the relationship was between tenant and landlord."

Suddenly, the former detective looked much more energetic. "I've been looking for another hobby. I'll see what I can find out."

I was very pleased to have Harry Bloom on my team. While I trusted Ian Chisholm completely, our relationship was just too complicated. Harry Bloom was much older, happily married, and had a lot of time on his hands. Also, unlike my vampires, he was awake during the same hours I was. A real plus in a sleuthing sidekick.

I was just about to leave Harry Bloom's house when my mobile rang. It was Mrs. Beasley. I hoped against hope that someone at the white elephant sale had fallen in love with the poodle lamp and she was begging for its return. I am nothing if not an optimist.

However, the minute I answered my phone and she spoke, I could tell she was calling about something much more serious than the world's ugliest lamp. When she said, "Lucy? Is that you?" Her voice trembled, and she sounded on the verge of tears.

"Yes, it's me. Is everything all right?" My fingers had started to tingle again, but I thought that was just empathy. Or fear. She had the kind of tone that people in horror movies have right before the monster rips their head off. We'd vanquished the soul-sucking demon who tried to take over my knitting shop some months ago, but that didn't mean there wasn't another one in the area. Though how would she know to call me?

"I found a watch." She huffed in and out a few times as though she were hyperventilating. "Could you come over and have a look at it?" There was so much unsaid in those few words. Now I understood the source of her fear. It wasn't a soul-sucking demon she was worried about. It was her husband and the possibility that he might have killed his stepfather.

I suspected that given the choice between a horrific monster and discovering the man she loved was a different kind of monster, she might've opted for the soul-sucking demon.

I didn't say any of that, of course. "Is your husband at home?"

Now she whispered, as though he might be in the other

room. "No. But I expect him within the hour. Please. Could you come to the house?"

Not only was I helpless against the appeal in her voice, but if she had that watch, then we had Robert Beasley. "I'll be right there."

Briefly I explained to Harry Bloom what was going on. Before I'd even finished speaking, he was pulling on his jacket. I felt the echo of his detective days, when a phone call might mean any number of disasters had befallen his town, and it was his job to solve mysteries, punish the guilty, and preserve the innocent. Rather unnecessarily given his actions, he said, "I'm coming with you."

Within two minutes, we were outside, and he locked the door of his cottage. I looked doubtfully at Gran's old Ford. "Do you want me to drive?" I asked, hoping very much he'd say no.

To my relief, he shook his head. "We'll walk across the fields. It's quicker, and Beasley won't be alerted if he comes home early by one of our cars sitting outside his house."

Not only did that make sense, but I was relieved not to have to drive. He strode to the end of his driveway, very quickly for a retired gentleman. We crossed the narrow road, climbed over a stile, and began walking across a farmer's field. I loved climbing over stiles. It was one of the English customs that I found most endearing. There were ancient rights-of-way all over the country, and private landowners just had to put up with people crossing their land. However, it also meant that the traveler had to contend with livestock. I wasn't a particularly nervous woman, but I didn't grow up with sheep and cows and Old McDonald's farm.

There were four or five cows in the field, and the way they glared at us, I did not think they knew about the ancient right-of-way thing. I scurried up until I was walking beside Harry Bloom. "Are those cows friendly?"

He looked down at me in some kindness. "They take some

getting used to, I admit. But most of the time, if you don't bother them, they don't bother you."

One cow seemed to be glaring at me particularly fiercely. I noticed that she had a calf standing beside her. "What do you mean most of the time?"

The mother cow took a couple of steps toward us, and I thought that if she just sat on me it would all be over. She must have weighed a thousand pounds. "The mothers do sometimes become a bit aggressive. It's the protective instinct."

Mama took another step toward me and glared. "She lowered her head. Is that bad?"

"If they charge us, the best thing to do is run like hell."

I should have insisted that we drive. I picked up the pace. There was another fence, and another stile, coming up. That cow seemed to be the leader of her small herd, and as she made her way toward us, so did the rest of them. I was feeling distinctly nervous now, and I suddenly realized that my London-born former cop was just as nervous as I was. We were walking so fast, the pair of us were breathing heavily. I had one eye on the advancing cows and another on the ground, where any number of cow-pats bulged like an obstacle course.

"I'm sure they're just curious," he panted. Gentleman that he was, he stood back and let me clamber over the stile first. I fell into the next field, and he landed right beside me. We stopped to take a breath and assess what new challenges lay ahead of us. Fortunately, this field appeared to be empty. "It's just over there," he said in an encouraging tone.

"Right," I said. They were only cows. What harm could they do? And then I heard a sound like a clump of wet mud being thrown against the side of a barn. I looked down and discovered that I had stepped right in the middle of a fresh cow pie. I tugged my foot free, but a lot of cow excrement came along with it.

"Come along. No time to waste."

He was right, so I didn't stop to scrape what I could off my shoe but rushed along trying to keep up.

Fortunately, this field led to the end of the lane, and down the lane was the Beasleys' home. Mrs. Beasley must've been watching for me, for I'd barely started up the path to the door when it flew open. "Lucy. I'm so glad you're here." She looked quite panicked. Her eyes were wide, her cheeks flushed, and her lips trembled. Then she saw Harry Bloom and took a step back into the house. "Oh."

I introduced Harry Bloom and explained that I had been with him when the call came. I said he knew quite a bit about antique watches. I didn't explain that he was a retired police officer because I didn't want her any more freaked out than she already was.

She looked doubtful, but what could she do? "Come in."

Out of respect for her beautiful home, I toed off my filthy shoes and left them outside, though I felt quite vulnerable coming into the home where a possible killer lived in nothing but stocking feet.

I could feel Harry Bloom's impatience. I had quite a bit of impatience myself, but I also could see that bringing an extra person had really thrown Mrs. Beasley. I said, as soothingly as I could, "Mr. Bloom is an expert on watches. You can trust him." She looked into my eyes, and while I tried not to use my magic to manipulate her, I said a little calming spell. Frankly, I needed it for myself as well as for her.

Her shoulders dropped down from around her ears, and her lips stopped trembling. "I'm sure I'm being foolish. I just— it looks so much like the one in that painting."

I knew that Harry Bloom wanted to question her, so I shot him a warning glance. I was pretty sure I could come up with most of the questions he wanted to ask her. "Where did you find it?"

She heaved a sigh. "Do you remember when I told you that

I'd taken some of his old bits and bobs and put them in the white elephant sale?"

"Of course I do."

"Well, he'd been quite cross with me and, naturally, once he said he didn't want those things sold, I gave him back the box to bring home. Just today I thought if these things were important to him, we should display them in some way. I thought I might get a little cabinet, and so I took the box out to have a look at what was inside it, and that's when I saw the watch."

"Was the watch inside that box when Mr. Beasley reclaimed it from the white elephant sale?"

She shook her head. There was a line of worry between her brows. "No. It was just some old lead soldiers and ancient wooden toys and, I don't know, rubbish, I'd have called it. I'm sure there was no watch."

"But there was one today?"

The worry frown deepened. "I suppose I'd better show you."

We followed her into the dining room, and there was the silver pocket watch sitting on the dining room table. She had the dining room lights all on, so it was clear that she had come in here in order to compare the watch with the one in the painting.

I drew closer, feeling the gloom of despair once more in that room. "May I?"

"I suppose so."

I picked it up. I knew the second I did that it was the same watch Elizabeth had shown me on the day she was killed. Still, I did my due diligence. I opened it. I looked at the hallmark symbols. And then I passed the watch to Harry Bloom. "This is the same watch Elizabeth showed me only minutes before she was killed."

CHAPTER 24

*M*rs. Beasley tottered as though she might faint and plopped herself down into one of the dining chairs. She didn't say anything, but I felt her pain and confusion and sorrow just as keenly as though she had screamed and wailed and cried out. I wanted to comfort her, but how could I? We'd just proven that her husband was a murderer. All I could really give her was confirmation that she'd done the right thing. "You did the only thing you could."

"There must be some mistake," she said in a small voice.

I thought the mistake was that Robert Beasley had hidden that watch in the same spot he'd kept it for so many years.

I felt sad for this woman, and her pain was like a physical presence in the room, but Harry Bloom was clearly delighted. He had the sense not to jump up and down and throw his fist in the air, but as easily as I could feel her pain, I could feel his triumph. However, he was an old pro, and all he said was, "We need to call the police."

Mrs. Beasley put her head in her hands, but she didn't argue. I pulled out my mobile, but before I could call anyone, a voice said, "What's going on in here?"

As Robert Beasley came into the dining room, his wife made a sound like a parched mouse trying to squeak. I supposed we'd been so busy studying that watch that none of us had heard him come in. Or else he'd come in with great stealth. No doubt he'd seen my shoes outside and knew perfectly well that I was here.

He glanced at me, and then he glanced at Harry Bloom, and his face hardened. "What are you doing here?"

And then his gaze fell on the watch in Harry Bloom's hand. Bloom turned, and the two men faced each other. We women might as well have been in a different country for all the attention they paid us. This was a very old standoff, and I felt the aggression from both of them.

Harry Bloom said, "I've been looking for this watch for a very long time."

Robert Beasley's color went beetroot and then paled to deathly white. "That's not what it looks like."

The urbane, petunia-planting, tea-making retired gentleman I had spent the day with was gone. Harry Bloom drew himself up taller, and his eyes were steely as Ian Chisholm's when he was about to arrest a murderer. "No? Tell me what it looks like."

Robert Beasley turned to his wife, who was staring at him through wide, scared eyes. He took a step toward her. "Darling. Surely you don't think I'd kill the only father I ever knew?"

Her voice was barely above a whisper. "Then where did the watch come from?"

"I found it." His gaze dropped, and he said those words the way a teenager might when they've been caught out in wrongdoing.

"You found it?" Harry Bloom's voice dripped with sarcasm. "Your father never let it out of his sight or his hand. I can only assume that you found it when you bludgeoned him to death."

We all shuddered at the way he described the murder, so

brutally. Robert Beasley reached for his wife's hand, but she pulled hers away before he could touch her and clutched her fingers in her lap.

He looked so sad. "No. I found it in the grate. There." He indicated the fireplace in the dining room, underneath the picture of his dead stepfather. "Months later, after he was dead. We barely used the dining room for obvious reasons. But Mother decided to have a dinner. I cleaned out the grate, and there it was."

Harry Bloom did not look convinced. "That's a heart-warming story. Why did you never bother to tell anyone?"

Robert Beasley backed up until he was leaning against the heavy mantle above the fireplace. "Because by that time, we'd already had the insurance money. That watch was worth quite a lot of money. If I admitted I'd found the watch, I would've had to give the insurance money back but, worst of all, I would've faced questions exactly like the ones you're throwing at me now." He looked like a man at the end of his rope. "I did not kill my stepfather. But that watch was very sentimental. I'd have liked to wear it as a memento, but I couldn't. So I kept it in my box of old treasures from childhood. Sometimes, when my wife was out and no one was expected, I used to wear it. For comfort."

Bloom wasn't buying it. "And then your wife found it and the box of what you call your boyhood treasures and put all the things up for sale in the white elephant booth at the village fête."

We all knew that was true, and Robert Beasley nodded. He didn't seem so sure of himself now. He stared down at the floor and, with the toe of his shoe, worried the edge of the British India carpet.

Harry Bloom said, "And Elizabeth Palmer bought that watch."

He didn't raise his head. He nodded again.

"Elizabeth showed that watch to Lucy here. She was very excited. It was going to be a gift for her husband to celebrate their twenty-fifth wedding anniversary. That's the silver anniversary," he said in a patronizing tone, as though Robert Beasley might not know this fact.

"And then within minutes of showing Lucy that watch, she was shot through the heart with an arrow. I believe you're quite a good archer, Mr. Beasley, aren't you?"

He raised his head now. "Me and half the county. Besides, why would I kill Elizabeth over a watch? She was a nice woman. I could've gone to her and explained the situation. She'd have let me buy it back from her. She was that sort."

"And yet, that watch wasn't with Elizabeth's body. Perhaps you can explain how it comes to be back with you?"

There was a dreadful moment of silence. Harry Bloom continued, "Because you saw Elizabeth with that watch, she was clearly showing everyone her new purchase. Someone was bound to recognize it eventually, so you slipped back here and got your bow and arrow and walked down the lane to the village hall. No one would see you. Everyone was at the fête. You crept up to the second floor, where you had a clear view of the village green, and you waited. All she had to do was come into view, and you had a clear shot."

"No."

"Once you shot her, there was bound to be chaos and panic, and you could stash your bow, ready to pick up later, run over to the fair, drop to your knees beside the body pretending to be one of the concerned friends and pick up that watch."

"I tell you I didn't kill her. I wouldn't." He looked at his wife again, but her hands were covering her face. "All right. I did see Elizabeth with that watch. I planned to talk to her quietly and see if I could buy it back. Before I had a chance to do that, she was killed." His eyes dropped back down to the carpet. "I admit I'm not proud of what happened next. It was in a paper bag.

When she was hit by the arrow, the bag was knocked out of her hand. I didn't even think. There was nothing I could do for Elizabeth. She wasn't going to need that watch anymore. Poor woman was never going to celebrate her wedding anniversary. The watch was mine anyway. My wife put it into the white elephant sale by mistake. I was only reclaiming my own property."

"Except that watch is the piece of evidence that ties you to the murder of your stepfather. And now to the murder of Elizabeth Palmer."

"No! I told you. I found that watch in the grate. It must have fallen in his struggle with the burglar."

"Robert. You've had thirty years to come up with a story. Is that really the best you can do?"

"It's the truth."

"Well, I don't believe you. And I doubt very much whether a judge and jury will believe you, either."

Mrs. Beasley began to sob noiselessly into her hands. I thought back to that map I'd seen. "You own the land that Jason and Elizabeth's house sits on, isn't that correct?"

Everyone looked to me now. I suppose it was a bit of a drastic change of subject, but somehow I was certain it was relevant. My fingers had been tingling when I saw that map.

"Yes. They were nice people."

"Did you try to get rid of them as tenants? Were they behind on their rent?"

"You don't understand. They own the house. I only own the land it sits on, by ancient right. I couldn't get rid of them as tenants if I wanted to. And I wouldn't want to. They were nice people."

He hadn't answered my second question. "We know that Jason was in bad financial trouble. Had he stopped paying the rent?"

He shrugged. "I hadn't raised that rent in years. It didn't

matter. After my father died, I sold land to anyone who wanted it. I'm not some feudal lord. Quite a number of our neighbors wanted to buy their land. Most of them were easy decisions, but it was a bit difficult to sell the fields to a developer who wanted to put in that subdivision. If it hadn't been a local man, I probably wouldn't have done it. Father would've turned in his grave. But"—here his eyes rose to contemplate the portrait of Grayson Timmins staring fiercely back—"he was a man who looked to the past. He wanted to keep things the way they'd always been. He'd never sell any of the land, and he refused to give permission to any landowner to expand their properties or add more outbuildings.

"He liked our village to remain peaceful and as it had always been, as though we were stuck in the nineteenth century. I expect he'd have disapproved of the train if he could've stopped it, but once it was here, he liked to make sure it ran on time." He shook his head. "But you can't stop progress. Besides, taxes were rising, and there were the death duties when he died. It made much more sense to sell the fields for subdivision, which would bring more people into the area and, as I said, I was only too happy to sell land to the locals who'd owned houses and farms for centuries."

Because I didn't know what else to say, I went with, "You must've made a lot of money."

"I hope I was reasonable. I tried to be. But yes, we've been able to live comfortably off the investments for years."

Harry Bloom took over. "That's all very interesting, Mr. Beasley. Perhaps you'd like to repeat all this down at the station."

He looked like a little boy who'd been caught out in mischief. "The station? Are you arresting me?"

"I'm not in the business of arresting people anymore." I thought he was quite disappointed that he had to say those words. "But I believe the detectives would be very interested in hearing how you came to have this watch in your possession."

Robert Beasley looked wildly toward the window, and I wondered if he might try to make a break for it, and then his shoulders slumped. "Fine."

Harry Bloom said, "Mrs. Beasley? May I use your telephone?"

She still couldn't speak. She nodded.

I wanted to leave. I really wanted to leave. I didn't particularly want the police to find me here; it would cause too many awkward questions. Especially if it was Ian Chisholm who showed up, as I suspected it would be, as he was the one investigating the cold case. But how could I leave poor Mrs. Beasley? She'd done the right thing, the brave thing, by calling me, and perhaps now she regretted it. She hadn't realized that I would come with the former police detective and that he would so quickly turn her husband over to the police.

And so I waited with her. It wasn't Ian who came after all, but DI Thomas. He didn't seem bothered that I was there. He was more interested in Harry Bloom and Robert Beasley. After the former detective had gone through his theory, Robert Beasley was taken away.

"Oh, what have I done?" Florence cried, burying her head in her hands once more.

"The right thing," I assured her. Though there'd been something very sincere in her husband's story. But good liars could always sound sincere.

CHAPTER 25

The next day in the shop, Violet was in a really good mood. In running a retail store, I'd discovered that a salesperson in a good mood sells a lot more than one who's grumpy and out of sorts. Violet sold nearly twice as much as she normally did, and that put me in a good mood as well.

One thing was puzzling me, though. The possibility that Robert Beasley was telling the truth. Okay, I admitted that it wasn't terribly likely, but what if he had found that watch in the grate? What if Jason Palmer got away with murder because of me and my interfering?

I was so bothered that I drove back to Harry Bloom's house and asked him to make me a copy of that map. He shook his head at me. "Lucy, you solved the case."

"But don't you think it's possible that Robert Beasley is telling the truth?"

He narrowed his eyes at me and shook his head. "No. Frankly I don't."

I'd found him watering his freshly planted petunias, and when he'd finished, he said, "Come on, then."

I followed him up to his office. Though he had a photocopier in the corner, after looking at his file for a moment, he picked the whole thing up and handed it to me. "Just make sure to return this when you're done. Not that I think I'll need it anymore. I just like to keep some of these for posterity."

"Do you really not think there is even the tiniest possibility that Robert Beasley might have been telling the truth?"

"Of course, there's always the tiniest possibility. Our job isn't to judge them. Lucy, our job is to gather sufficient evidence so that a judge and jury can debate the facts, with the help of highly priced solicitors and barristers of course, and try to determine that justice is done."

"But two days ago, we were convinced Jason Palmer had killed his wife."

"And perhaps he did. And perhaps Robert Beasley killed his stepfather."

"Two murders by two separate killers?" I asked.

"Or Robert Beasley killed them both. As I said before, we've done our job."

He seemed to forget that my job was to run a knitting shop. This other gig I'd picked up was clearly a side hustle, and I wasn't entirely sure I was so good at it. Or that he wasn't letting thirty years of frustration influence his opinion.

However, I didn't feel like hanging around and arguing with him in case he decided to take that precious folder back again. I thanked him and returned to my shop. I took the folder upstairs. Since I had to go to Joanna's farmhouse that night for the Friday knit-in and Scarlett was helping out in the shop that afternoon, I slipped upstairs for a couple of hours of peace and quiet.

I was very fond of my cousin Violet, but I would be really glad when she was gone and I had the place to myself again. Well, alone apart from the vampires who seemed to come and go as though this was their clubhouse.

I opened the folder and began going through each piece of

paper once more. I knew that Harry Bloom was right and there was a very efficient justice system, but I also knew that justice was blind. I had two perfectly good eyes, and I was determined to use them so that the wrong person wasn't convicted of a murder they hadn't committed. Double points to me if the right person was convicted.

CHAPTER 26

J was poring over the map as though secrets might be revealed to me if I stared at it long enough. But it was a like a geometry puzzle. And I was never any good at geometry. I don't know how long I'd have studied that map feeling as though I was missing something if Nyx hadn't jumped up and meowed in my face. That pulled me out of my reverie and made me look at the clock. Dinnertime.

I got up and stretched out my aching back, opened a can of her favorite tuna and put it in the dish and then freshened her water. While she sat daintily munching, I decided to be a good cousin and make dinner for Violet and me. I wasn't the world's greatest cook, but I thought I could manage something simple. I opened the freezer and stared inside.

There were the frozen salmon fillets I had picked up the other day when I felt like I needed to eat more healthy. Of course, they needed to be thawed, and I didn't have much time.

I closed the freezer and opened the fridge. That was pretty dismal, unless we wanted eggs and yogurt and broccoli for dinner. Maybe walking up to the store would be good for me. It would get me some air, plus I could buy some fresh food or even better, that wonderful invention, the ready meal.

As I was getting ready to go, my buzzer rang, and to my surprise, it was Rafe. I let him in and, to my joy, he carried an insulated food bag—the sort that takeout drivers use, only this one was much nicer, designed, I supposed, for high-end picnics.

"This is a surprise."

As was the mouthwatering fragrance emanating from the food bag.

"William doesn't think you eat properly."

I took instant offense, telling him that at that very moment I had salmon fillets in the freezer and broccoli in the fridge. I didn't argue very hard, though, as the last thing I wanted was for him to take that delicious-smelling food away again.

He gave a half-smile thing, which I always interpreted as his attempt not to laugh in my face. "William really wanted the excuse to cook. He knows your cousin's here with you, so there's plenty for two."

It was kind of Rafe's housekeeper to think of us and kind of Rafe to bring the food with him. "Do you want to stay and join us?"

"Thanks. I've already eaten."

He carried food into the kitchen and put the bag on the counter. I immediately unzipped it to see what was inside. When I opened the lid, the delicious smells were even more delicious. "This smells amazing."

He leaned over the bag, and his sensitive nose quivered. "It's a coq au vin. And I'm going to have to talk to William about using the good burgundy in a chicken stew."

I couldn't believe this guy. "You have to be messing with me. You can't seriously tell what kind of wine he used?"

He looked rather offended at that. "Of course I can. I have an excellent sense of smell. Also an excellent palate." He closed his eyes and said, "The herbs are tarragon, rosemary, parsley and thyme from the kitchen garden. I think William grew the garlic. The mushrooms and onions and celery have obviously come from the market. And that chicken is organic."

"Seriously, now you're just messing with me."

He looked down at me, and his eyes glinted. "Am I?"

I didn't think we were talking about food anymore, and my stomach fluttered. Rafe got to me in a deep and elemental way. One day I was going to figure out what on earth I was supposed to do about this strong attraction. But not today.

Rafe hefted the weighty Le Creuset casserole dish out of the bag and slipped it into the oven, which I put on a low heat. Apart from the chicken was a dish of roast potatoes, a fresh loaf of bread, a salad and a half bottle of wine. Inside was a note.

Dear Lucy,

Please don't be offended. My talents are so wasted on Rafe. Enjoy the simple meal.

Cheers, William

P.S. Tell Rafe the rule of good cooks is that you should never cook with a wine you wouldn't drink.

While I was fussing in the kitchen, Rafe wandered over to the map, which I'd spread out on the dining table. "I heard that you found the missing pocket watch. Well done, Lucy."

"I'd love to take credit for it, but it was Mrs. Beasley who found it. It freaked her out, and she called me."

"I imagine it would be disturbing, discovering one's loved one was most likely a murderer."

Before I could tell him about my suspicions that Robert Beasley might be telling the truth, Vi came upstairs and sniffed the air. "What smells so good?"

"Rafe and William are treating us to dinner."

"Fabulous. Can we eat soon? Sylvia suggested that I come and help with her lesson tonight instead of you."

I thought about the very reason she was staying with me. "Are you sure that's wise?"

She put her head to one side, looking decidedly pleased with herself. "Lucy. The murders have been solved. That's why Sylvia thinks I should go tonight. Nobody's going to accuse me of being a witch anymore. And when they see me helping them out with their knitting, we'll be friends again."

I thought Sylvia was onto something. Besides, if I didn't have to go to the knitting class tonight, I could spend the evening studying Harry Bloom's file. Maybe Robert Beasley had killed his stepfather and then murdered Elizabeth to get that watch back, and maybe he'd killed Grayson Timmins and Jason Palmer had killed Elizabeth.

I just had a feeling that something was wrong. Or maybe I wanted to avoid attending a knitting class pretending I knew what I was doing. "That's very smart of Sylvia. Promise you won't cast any spells on anybody, even though I know you're going to want to."

She laughed. "That's exactly what Sylvia said. I promise."

When she left, Rafe helped me with the dishes, which I thought was very nice of him considering he hadn't eaten anything, though he had drunk a glass of that nice wine.

My mind drifted back to the night before. "I'm not convinced. Yes, I know the evidence is compelling, but he told me that he discovered the watch in the fire grate a few months after the murder. He didn't come forward because, obviously, he knew Harry Bloom and the police were after him, but also he'd already received the insurance money. Okay, it doesn't make him look like a hero, but not giving back insurance money and murder are a long way apart from each other."

"But he then took that watch from Elizabeth Palmer. It seems logical to assume that he killed her to prevent anyone finding out he'd had that watch all those years. Because in a town like Moreton-Under-Wychwood, where everyone knows everyone else's business, someone was bound to recognize that watch. Grayson Timmins's portrait was on display in the dining room for anyone to see," Rafe said.

"You're right!" Why hadn't I thought of that before? "Why would he keep that painting on display?" I dried my wet hands and walked into the living room. Rafe followed. "If Robert Beasley murdered his stepfather and kept the watch, wouldn't he have put that painting away somewhere?"

"Who knows? If he was obsessed with hatred enough to murder the man and keep the watch as a souvenir, he might well have wanted to look at that picture every day as a reminder of his act of destruction."

I shuddered. "Or he didn't do it."

Unlike Harry Bloom, Rafe was at least open to other possibilities. "All right. If Robert Beasley didn't kill his father and Elizabeth, then who did?"

That was the sticking point. I had absolutely no idea. I settled myself at the dining table and stared at that map as I had been doing on and off all day. Rafe sat across from me. Nyx, always happy to see Rafe, jumped up onto his lap and then decided his silk necktie, which looked like Hermes, was really a cat toy.

She began to bat at the tie with her paw until, laughing, he picked her up and put her onto the floor. My cat, however, was not one to be ignored. She walked around to me, jumped up on my lap, and since I wasn't wearing any designer clothing she could ruin, she jumped up onto the table.

"Nyx," I scolded her. "You know you're not allowed on the table." We seemed to have a constant battle over who had all the power in this household. I tried to argue that I was in charge, but we both knew that wasn't true. She easily evaded my attempts to pick her up and instead trod daintily into the middle of the map. She then sat down, her tail curled around her and twitching slightly at the end. Then she stared down at that map as though it were a goldfish pond and she were tracking the movement of some fat, tasty-looking koi.

She was so adorable I didn't have the heart to push her off. Then she looked at me, and her eyes narrowed and opened as though she was trying to communicate with me. Was she hungry, thirsty, too hot or, like Rafe, was she just messing with me?

She reached forward with her paw and tapped an area of the map. It was in an area outside of town. Not near Elizabeth's house or the Beasleys'.

She looked up at me, and I swear she rolled her eyes. Then she patted the same spot again, quite sternly this time.

I stared at the map again, this time with new eyes. I let out a gasp. "Nyx, you are such a clever cat."

She yawned, bathing me in tuna breath. I could tell that Rafe had followed my line of thinking. Our gazes connected, and I said, "We need to go and see Jason."

He nodded. "I'll drive."

I only stopped to brush my teeth and grab my bag, and then with a final pat for Nyx, I ran out the door. I was very happy not to have to navigate these roads in the dark and have Rafe drive me.

When we got to the Palmers' house, I could see lights on, though it took ages before Jason answered the door. He looked disheveled, and his shirt was done up wrong. "I'm so sorry. Did I catch you napping?"

He looked very uncomfortable. "No. Not at all. It's Lucy, isn't it?" He tried to pull up a professional smile. It looked like being suspected of murder had really messed him up. "No doubt you're here about the car. It was a good idea to catch me at home."

Rafe said smoothly, "We do have a couple of questions. Could we come inside?"

"Of course."

I walked into the living room and discovered why his hair was disheveled and his shirt buttoned all wrong. Nora was sitting on the sofa, also looking somewhat disheveled, trying to look unconcerned. A bottle of red wine sat on the coffee table with two partly filled glasses.

It would've been amusing catching them in the act if her best friend and his wife hadn't been murdered so recently. Jason told Nora that we'd stopped by about a car, but she did not look convinced. She looked at me with suspicion. Smart woman.

She said, "Why aren't you at the knitting class?"

I could have asked her the same question, but I told her my assistant was taking my place.

Rafe remained by the doorway, leaving me to ask the questions. I couldn't find a diplomatic way to start, so I blurted out the question I needed answered. "Actually, we're not here about a car. I need to know who lent you money after the banks turned you down for your last loan."

Nora jumped up, furious. "That is none of your business, you nosy—"

Jason wasn't so quick to take offense. He knew better than anyone that the police were gathering evidence against him, hoping to arrest him for his wife's murder. "What's it got to do with you? I assure you, the dealership's safe. You'll get your car."

"Jason, I'm trying to help you."

Nora looked like she wanted to throw me out of the house. If Rafe hadn't been standing there, I thought she might have tried. "Don't trust her, Jase. Remember, she was the last person to talk to Elizabeth before she died."

"Nora, go and make us some coffee, will you?"

She glared at all of us before stomping out of the room.

He ran a hand through his hair, but it was such a mess, it didn't really make any difference. I imagined it was a nervous gesture rather than a grooming one. He gestured to the wine. "I know this doesn't look good, but—"

"I really don't care about your love life or your morals. I'm trying to find the truth."

His jaw went slack and he stared as though he couldn't believe I'd said those words to his face. "How do you know I needed a loan?"

Rafe had left me to ask the difficult question, so I tossed a little discomfort his way. "Rafe didn't want me putting down a deposit on a car until he'd checked out your business. He has sources. It's true you were in financial difficulties, isn't it? And that the bank refused to give you any more money, so you had to get private financing?"

Slowly, he nodded. He gazed at Rafe. Everyone around here must know he was rich. Maybe Jason thought Rafe wanted to bail him out or buy his business or something. I thought the longer he thought that, the more likely he'd be to cooperate.

"We need to know who made you that loan and how much it was for."

He glanced at the hallway as though making sure Nora couldn't hear us. "Look, it's very embarrassing. Nora doesn't know anything about this."

We waited.

And then, with a great sigh, he told us.

Sometimes being right could really suck.

CHAPTER 27

$\mathcal{R}$afe backed out of the drive so fast, gravel spurted. He drove back toward the village as though he were in the final lap of the Grand Prix.

We reached the village. An old man was crossing the High Street, walking an arthritic dog. Glaciers retreated faster than these two could cross the road. "Come on, come on," Rafe said under his breath.

Finally they reached the other side, and we pressed on. We flew past the sign that said Nickleby Farm and set the hanging baskets swinging.

The lights were all on in the farmhouse where the knitting class was taking place.

I opened the door before the car came to a halt. "You stay here," I said to Rafe. "I'll call you if I need you."

"Be careful."

I wished I'd brought a bag of knitting. I hadn't, so I headed for the door empty-handed. I tried to put a calm, pleasant expression on my face as I opened the farmhouse door. It wasn't locked.

Sylvia had finished her lesson and the class was knitting

away. Joanna rose, looking delighted when she saw me. "Lucy. Violet said you wouldn't be coming tonight. We are so pleased you changed your mind."

Violet looked quite surprised to see me too. "I wasn't sure I'd be able to make it," I said. "What did I miss?"

Sylvia sent me a suspicious look but said nothing. One of the busily knitting women looked up. I remembered her from last week. She was the gossip. "We were talking about poor Florence Beasley. She didn't come tonight. Didn't have the heart for it. The police have been questioning him, you know. They think he killed his father. Well, stepfather I suppose."

No doubt Florence Beasley didn't relish being among a bunch of gossips in her darkest hour. Needles clacking, the gossipy woman knitted on. "Who'd have thought it? Robert Beasley was a nice man, we always thought. But then, so was Jason Palmer. Though I never liked the look of him. I'm only pleased to say I never bought a car from Jason Palmer. He might not have killed his wife, but as for him carrying on with Nora Betts, which everyone knows he is, and his wife barely cold, it's shocking, that's what I call it. Shocking."

The door opened, and in came Joanna's husband. Joanna rose and headed toward where he stood, just inside the door. "Bill? What are you doing here? We've got knitting classes tonight. I'm sure I told you."

Bill Newman looked like a well-to-do retiree. He wore a short-sleeved cotton shirt, dark trousers and polished loafers. His white hair was well-cut over a face that must once have been hand-some. He looked a little embarrassed to find twenty-odd women staring at him and also confused. He held a yellow plastic flash-light in his hand. "I got a phone call at the house. The message was that you wanted me to come down." He gestured with the flashlight. "I thought maybe a fuse had blown." But the lights were all burning perfectly well. "Didn't you want me?"

"No."

I laughed, I hoped convincingly. "Oh, Mr. Newman. It was me who wanted to see you. There must've been some mistake when the message was relayed to you. You see, I'm planning to buy a car from Jason Palmer. But with everything that's going on, I want your word that you won't call in his loan before I've got my car."

The man looked quite taken aback. "Perhaps you'd like to come up to the house. We don't want to interrupt the class."

Too late. Every ear was turned our way. "Oh, it's all right. Jason told me all about it. How generous you've been to him. Lending him the money to keep his business afloat when the banks wouldn't lend him any more money. It was so generous of you to help him."

The man glanced nervously at his wife and then back to me. "I was only being neighborly. I'm sure he wouldn't want us to be talking about him in this way."

Jason might not want to be talked about, but I could tell most of the women here were dying to hear the rest. Every single knitting needle had stopped moving, and we had everyone's attention.

I said, "If Jason goes to jail, he'll have to declare bankruptcy, and you'll never be repaid. That would hurt, at your age. It's not like you can earn more money."

He walked farther into the room. "We're very much hoping he won't be arrested. I'm sure he wouldn't hurt anyone. But I didn't lend him the money, you see. It was for Elizabeth." He looked truly sad. "I've known Elizabeth since she was a child. I hated to think of her losing her home and finding out what a terrible businessman her husband was, this year of all years, when they were celebrating twenty-five years of marriage. It was only a temporary loan to tide him over. He promised me things would get better."

"But they weren't getting better, were they? He was going down, and he was going to take you with him."

Joanna had been standing sort of stunned, but suddenly, like a puppet whose master pulled the strings again, she sprang to life. "Lucy. Please. This is a knitting class. If you don't have any knitting to do, perhaps you should leave."

Her super-nice act was faltering and badly. I looked at her. "And I thought you were being neighborly when you sided with Nora in jumping to Jason's defense. Gathering these women here to prove him innocent. But you knew Jason hadn't killed Elizabeth, didn't you? And if he was convicted of her murder, he wouldn't get the million pounds in life insurance. And if he didn't get the insurance money, then you wouldn't get the loan paid back. The loan that your generous husband so foolishly gave him."

Her lips pressed tightly together as though she were holding back a torrent of words. "This is ridiculous. And extremely rude. I think we'll have to end this meeting early. I'm very sorry, everyone."

No one moved. The gossipy woman looked at us agog. "Are you saying that Bill here had something to do with Elizabeth's death?"

He seemed completely taken aback. "I was helping at the pie stand. I didn't even know she was dead until someone from the band came and told us."

"And besides, you're not the archer in your family, are you?"

He shook his head. "No. My eyes aren't good enough."

I pulled the brochure about corporate retreats from my bag. I opened it and pointed to the relevant passage. "But at Nickleby Farm you offer archery, along with other activities like horseback riding, golf, and croquet."

The poor man looked as though he needed to sit down. He said, "I take people fishing and golfing."

Joanna looked desperate. "Shut up, you fool. Go back home. I'll be there in a minute."

We all stared at her in shock. The lovely, sweet-tempered woman shrieking at her husband. He didn't look shocked, though. He looked as though he was used to it.

Sylvia said, "Lucy, what are you suggesting? Do you think that Joanna and her husband had something to do with Elizabeth's death?"

I looked at Joanna. "I think Joanna had everything to do with it. You teach archery; it says so right in your corporate brochure. It would have been so easy for you to slip upstairs in the village hall and wait. Everyone was at that fair. You could take your time, wait until you got a clear shot at Elizabeth. Who'd suspect you? Her husband was having an affair. Her best friend wanted her out of the way so she could marry Jason. Even Nora's husband had a plausible motive. You were the first person who told me that he'd do anything for his wife. You made me think he might've killed Elizabeth so that Nora and Jason could be happy together. That was clever of you."

"I don't know what you've been smoking, but I do not let anyone come into my house and insult me or my husband. I'm asking you again to leave."

I looked at the other women gathered there. "Do you want me to leave? Or do you think we should look at some of the other facts?"

Her hand was shaking, and she was barely in control. "If you don't get out of here, I'm calling the police."

I laughed. "I think that's an excellent idea."

She all but shook her fist. "It was Robert Beasley. The police have arrested him, you stupid cow."

"And wasn't that convenient for you?" I asked in amazement. "You had no idea when you killed Elizabeth that she was holding evidence that implicated Robert Beasley, not only in her death but in his father's. That's what finally led me to you. I was trying to make a connection between Robert Beasley and Elizabeth, and that's how I found out that his family had owned all this land around here. Including this farm."

"So what? If you were from this country, you would know that land leases are common."

"I've learned a bit about land leases recently. You retired to Moreton-Under-Wychwood with all your grand plans to build this corporate retreat. It was your retirement business, your last chance to make some money, but you needed Grayson Timmins's permission to dig a swimming pool or chop down old trees or build any outbuildings. And your landlord said no."

"This is ridiculous."

"Robert Beasley told me himself that his stepfather wanted everything in the village to remain just as it was. He didn't want new businesses, and he must have hated the very idea of corporate retreats. Why did you go to see him that day? Did you hope to convince him to let you have your way? Did you beg? Because you needed the money, didn't you? Even then? Your husband's always been too generous. Without this business, you were going to be in trouble."

"Bill, can't you do something?"

But he sat quietly, watching me.

"I think you went to see Grayson Timmins and plead your case one last time. Did you plan to kill him? Or was it an act of passion? Were you in a blind rage when you picked up that heavy candlestick and bashed him over the head with it?"

"Stop talking!" She was showing us all what she looked like in a blind rage.

"Once you'd killed him, you didn't panic. You stole some valuables to make it look like a burglary."

She was gasping like a fish now. "It wasn't me. It was Robert Beasley. Ask the police."

"Robert Beasley saved you. Once Grayson Timmins was dead, his wife and seventeen-year-old son took over. It was a new era. They were happy to sell you the land at a cheap price. And things were all right for a while. Your business was successful, and with your husband out of London, you thought he'd stop being so foolish with the money. Until you found out your husband had given Jason Palmer a private loan. Jason was going bankrupt, and he was going to take you with him."

"That's not true."

"Until you found out about that million-pound life insurance policy. Poor Elizabeth never knew what hit her."

"This is absolute nonsense. It's a fantasy story you've invented. You haven't got a shred of proof, because there isn't any."

She had me there. I had hoped attacking her in front of all these women might provoke her into confessing. But a woman who would calmly murder a neighbor was not so easily rattled.

Bill Newman finally said, "Joanna? Is this true? Did you kill Elizabeth for money?"

"Of course I didn't."

He heaved a great sigh. "You did kill Grayson Timmins, though."

"What?" She turned on him, now, murder in her eye.

He took a step back but continued, "I've always known it. Never wanted to tackle you with it because I loved you, you see. Maybe Grayson Timmins was wrong, holding this village back in the Dark Ages. I knew you'd gone to see him the day he was killed, but I always believed it was an accident and you were sorry. It never happened again, and so I let myself believe it was an aberration." He shook his head. "But killing Elizabeth Palmer was deliberate. That was cruel."

She let out a shriek. "You're as crazy as she is."

He shook his head again. "I know where she hid those things she stole from Mr. Timmins. For thirty years I've known. I can't prove that my wife killed Elizabeth Palmer, but I can give you the proof that she murdered Grayson Timmins."

Joanna was fast, I'll give her that. She flew toward the door, shoving her husband out of the way, no doubt intending to get rid of the evidence. I was so startled, she was out the door before I could make my feet move. Sylvia passed me, but still Joanna had the door open and was running outside. She gave a shriek as she slammed into Rafe. He grabbed her arm and dragged her back inside, struggling. He looked to me and gave me a tiny nod. "I don't think you've finished with your meeting."

Sylvia said, "I suppose someone should call the police."

Rafe said, "I took the liberty."

CHAPTER 28

*J*une the twenty-first was as sunny and bright as the longest day of the year should be. It was Friday morning, and Violet, now thankfully living back in her own cottage, arrived early with takeout coffee and muffins, one of which had a birthday candle in it. She said, "No wonder you're such a powerful witch, with your birthday falling on the summer solstice."

"I've always loved having my birthday on the longest day of the year. I get to enjoy the day longer."

"I hope you don't mind that tonight we're having dinner with our grandmothers. I was thinking maybe we'd go to the pub afterward and meet up with some of the girls, give you a proper celebration on your twenty-eighth birthday."

Her tone was altogether too airy. I knew something more was planned than a simple family dinner. The vampires had been going around very secretive and full of suppressed excitement. Conversations had ended abruptly when I entered a room. They might be superhuman, but they were terrible at planning a surprise party. Still, I played along because it was so sweet that they wanted to do something nice for me.

"That would be great." I was making friends here in Oxford. It was nice to know that I knew enough people for a party.

Late that morning, Ian Chisholm came into the shop and, looking sheepish, said, "Happy Birthday, Lucy." He handed me a card that read, "Happy Birthday to a very good friend. With love, Ian." After dating briefly, could we ever really go back to friends? I decided that was a question for another day. This day was all about me. Though I did ask him how the case against Joanna Newman was coming along.

"I never call a case airtight, but this one's close," he said with satisfaction. "Her fingerprints were all over the property stolen from Grayson Timmins the day he was murdered. She'd hidden the items in an old shed on Nickleby Farm. They were stuffed inside an old burlap sack of horse feed. It's more difficult to tie her to Elizabeth Palmer's murder, but her bow fits as the murder weapon, and she uses the same arrows as the one that killed Elizabeth."

"Good. It's time she paid for what she did."

I didn't see too much of the vampires that day. I expected they were all sleeping. Violet had arranged a dinner with the two of us and Scarlett and Polly. Gran couldn't be seen in public, but she was going to come to the flat later to hear about my evening and drink a glass of sherry with me. I noticed Violet kept glancing at her watch, and she kept checking her phone and texting when she thought I wasn't looking. Of course I pretended I didn't notice. We closed up as usual at five, and then she said, "Do you mind if I come upstairs to your place to change?"

"All right."

She brought a dress bag upstairs, and I was surprised at how fancy her blue frock was. She said, "I thought it would be fun to dress up. In honor of you making my village safe for witches once more, we're going to a very nice restaurant."

"All right." I could feel her suppressed excitement, and it

ignited mine. I pulled out a pink and white strapless dress and pink high-heeled sandals. In case it grew chilly, I slipped the white pashmina around my shoulders that I hadn't worn since the village fête. I put extra effort into my hair and makeup. When we were both ready, I asked, "Do you mind driving?"

"Sorry, Lucy. I would, but my car had a flat tire this morning. I had to get a ride to work. I was hoping you could drive."

I tried not to be irritated. "Perhaps we should take a cab?"

"Oh, come on," she chided. "If you drink too much, we'll get a taxi back. Or I can drive."

"Fine," I said, a little huffy, grabbing some sneakers to drive in. When we got to the spot where I'd wedged Gran's tiny car last time I drove it, I saw a brand-new car sitting there. The same model I'd test-driven, only this one was red. As bright and shiny as a fresh cherry. My jaw dropped. "I don't understand."

Violet started to laugh, and then the back doors of the car opened and Gran and Sylvia came out, both giggling and crying, "Happy Birthday!" We hugged, and I think I squealed. Gran said, "This is a gift from all of us. Rafe said you liked this car when you drove it."

Trust Rafe. He'd been right, though.

"Jason Palmer gave us a very good price, and he's promised you free servicing and oil changes for the rest of your natural life."

I stroked my new car. I was already in love. "Well, I did help save him from jail for a murder he didn't commit."

Sylvia nodded. "And that dreadful Joanna woman will soon be behind bars, where she should have been for the last thirty years." She shook her head. "Her poor husband. I don't know if Bill Newman will ever recover from the shock. He blames himself, you know. He had a great fondness for Elizabeth. That's why he lent her husband the money. If he hadn't made that loan, she'd still be alive. Bankrupt, but alive. He feels it badly. In protecting his wife all those years, he gave her the opportunity to kill Elizabeth."

I hugged the two vampires and then Violet and I piled into my brand-new car. While the roads didn't magically become right-hand drive, I had so much easier a time driving an automatic car that was smooth and responsive to the touch that I felt like I might actually enjoy driving again.

As we drove, I said, "You were right in your fortune-telling. Elizabeth did die. And, I guess now Jason's in the clear for murder, he'll get that check and marry Nora."

She shuddered. "I will never tell fortunes again." Then she brightened. "But I did do some good, you know. You remember that woman with low self-esteem whose dates canceled on her?"

"Of course. She was convinced you were a wicked witch."

"Well, guess who's got herself a new haircut, a better attitude, and a new beau?"

I was so astonished I took my eyes off the road for a second to stare at my witch cousin. "Are you kidding me? Who?"

She chuckled. "She's been having coffee with Tony Betts."

I felt the rightness of them together in my heart. "That's just perfect. I hope they'll be happy together."

"She couldn't be a worse partner than Nora."

There was that.

I kept following Violet's instructions, and then the scenery began to grow familiar. "Wait a minute. Where are we headed?"

But by then, I knew. We turned in to the open gates to Rafe's manor house. I pulled up in front of the house, or as close as I could get considering how many cars were already parked there.

As we got out, I heard a shriek and looked up to see Henri the peacock on top of his favorite wall. As I looked up at him, he fanned open his tail. I laughed at him in delight. "Thank you, Henri. I love you too."

The door opened. William said, "Good evening, ladies. Please come in. Happy Birthday, Lucy."

Rafe and his staff had gone all-out. There were pink and purple balloons everywhere and a garden party outside. As I wandered around, I realized how many friends I'd made here. There were Alice and Charlie from Frogg's Books holding hands and looking so deeply in love, I was expecting a wedding invitation any day now.

A group of theater students from Cardinal College stood in a laughing group. I was Happy Birthday'd and hugged by Scarlett and Polly, then Liam, who spent the rest of the evening flirting with my cousin Violet.

A few witches showed up, though they were on their way to the summer solstice celebration at the standing stones. I was so happy to have a good excuse not to go. Margaret Twig wished me a happy birthday and somehow managed to make the words sound vaguely like a threat. I didn't think she was here to celebrate the anniversary of my birth. I thought she was here for the free champagne.

Some of my favorite customers were there and, of course, most of the vampires. Rafe had organized a huge marquee tent so no one had to stand in the sunshine who didn't want to. Even so, many of the vampires chose to stay inside. I drank champagne and ate far too much of the gorgeous food.

Rafe was the perfect host, introducing people to each other here, making a laughing comment there, and never quite in my vicinity. The sun went down and the garden began to sparkle with twinkle lights and candles.

It was such a clear night, I felt that I could see every star in the heavens. From the squawking, I knew the peacocks were close by. Soon they'd be bedding down for the night. Rafe had once said that Henri was partial to steak. I helped myself to some of the sliced beef from the buffet table and slipped out, looking for my peacock boyfriend.

I headed for Henri's favorite spot and gasped when I saw a tall, dark shadow standing by the wall. Then I realized Rafe was on the same errand. "No wonder Henri's so fat," I scolded. "You keep feeding him."

"And what might you be doing out here with that napkin in your hand?" His voice was low and sexy.

I chuckled. "Busted."

Having heard voices, Henri waddled out as though we'd rung the dinner bell. Two other peacocks headed toward us and one of the peahens. I put down the food that I'd brought, and then Rafe pulled out a handkerchief and offered it to me so I could wipe my hands.

He stood beside me, and we both looked up at the stars. "How does it feel to be twenty-eight?"

I thought about his question. "Like I should be all grown up. Like I should know more by now."

He put an arm around my shoulders, and we stood there watching the peacocks enjoy their impromptu feast. "There's plenty of time to know everything."

"What were you doing on your twenty-eighth birthday?" Normally he didn't talk too much about his past, but I thought given that it was my birthday, he might throw me a bone. He seemed to be looking back into his past, and he had a long way to look. "That was the year Queen Elizabeth was crowned." He gave me a look. "I mean, of course, the first Queen Elizabeth. I spent many years in her service."

"Man, you are really old."

He looked down at me. "Old enough to know when you're trying to get a rise out of me."

I leaned into him. "Thank you for that beautiful car. I know it was your idea."

He didn't deny it. "I like to keep you safe. I was sure that old wreck of your grandmother's would leave you stranded somewhere."

"Do you want to take a ride?"

"What, now?"

"It's a beautiful night for a drive."

"And leave my guests?"

"Rafe, you've got a perfectly good staff. We won't be gone for long."

"Where are we going?"

"The standing stones."

"I thought you'd sworn off those witchy get-togethers."

I thought I had too. "Now that I'm all grown up, I think I'd better start taking this witch thing more seriously."

We walked toward my new car, and he said, "You're more powerful than you think." And then, so softly I could pretend I hadn't heard him, he said, "You've certainly bewitched me."

Thanks for reading *Fair Isle and Fortunes*. In her next adventure, Lucy's thrilled when a famous knitwear designer chooses her shop for a televised knitting class. Disaster hits when someone dies and she has to solve the crime before the cameras stop rolling. *Lace and Lies* is one click away.

A Note from Nancy

Dear Reader,

Thank you for reading the Vampire Knitting Club series. I am so grateful for all the enthusiasm this series has received. I have plenty more stories about Lucy and her undead knitters planned for the future.

I hope you'll consider leaving a review and please tell your friends who like cozy mysteries.

Review on Amazon, Goodreads or BookBub.

Your support is the wool that helps me knit up these yarns. Turn the page for a sneak peek of *Lace and Lies*, Book 7 of the Vampire Knitting Club.

I hope to see you in my private Facebook Group. It's a lot of fun. www.facebook.com/groups/NancyWarrenKnitwits

Until next time,
Happy Reading,

Nancy

LACE AND LIES

© 2019 NANCY WARREN

CHAPTER 1

"Teddy Lamont is coming to Cardinal Woolsey's." I was so excited I squeaked. Nineteen vampires stopped knitting, crocheting or gossiping to stare at me in various attitudes of awe. I'd saved the news so my grandmother would be among the first to hear it and for me to see her lined face beam with pleasure.

Gran had started Cardinal Woolsey's knitting and yarn shop and, even though she was now undead, I still liked to include her in all business decisions. She'd agreed with my idea to offer our shop for a special promotion by Larch Wools. Larch was making a TV series featuring celebrity sweater designer and knitting expert Teddy Lamont, who would teach one of his sweater patterns to a class inside a knitting shop.

Every knitting shop in the UK that carried Larch Wools had been invited to apply for the coveted spot. According to the letter I'd received, Cardinal Woolsey's was chosen for several reasons. We sold a lot of Larch Wools, Oxford was geographically in the middle of the UK, and the shop itself was photogenic and had room for a TV crew.

Several voices called out at once:

"When is it?"

"Can we all meet Teddy?"

"When will it be on the telly?"

I could only answer the first of these questions. "Filming takes place in a couple of weeks."

"So soon." Sylvia spoke up. She'd been a silent film star in the 1920s and based on that thought she knew everything about the entertainment industry. She looked me up and down critically. "You'll want to lose a few pounds, Lucy. The camera is unforgiving. And what will you wear? Hand knitted items, of course, but of the highest possible quality."

All the vampires listened intently. Alfred, who may not have been a movie star but was as bossy as Sylvia, chimed in. "Yes. There's no time to waste. If we all get started now, we can have an entire television wardrobe for Lucy by the time shooting starts."

"I don't need a new wardrobe," I protested. My closets and drawers were already overflowing with hand knitted garments from the vampires who soothed their boredom by knitting me the most exquisite creations. The weight loss, however, was probably a good idea. Working in a knitting shop wasn't conducive to an active lifestyle. At least, that's what I told myself.

Sylvia eyed my long blonde hair, which I'd stuck in a pony today since I was too lazy to style it. "You'll want to wear your hair back for the filming, so the camera can see your face." She shook her head in fond reminiscence. "What a time I had of it playing Lady Godiva. Sir John Barrymore was beside himself trying to keep my face visible to the camera and preserve my modesty."

Normally, I loved Sylvia's trips down her cinematic memory

lane, but today I was more interested in the upcoming televised knitting show than her long ago triumphs.

"Who will be in your class, dear?" Gran asked, perhaps also feeling we should get back on track.

"The yarn company is choosing the students. They're running a national contest. Six lucky winners get to learn from Teddy Lamont. If they don't live within driving distance, they'll be put up at a hotel for the few days we're filming."

"My goodness. They're going all out."

I was both excited and nervous. In knitting terms, this was like having a movie star come to your house for dinner.

"How typical," Hester moaned. Hester was perpetually a hormone-challenged teenager whose awkward stage would last for eternity. I tried to feel sympathy for her, remembering the misery of my own teenage years, but she made it difficult. "Maybe I would have liked to be in the class, but oh, no. Everything gets decided by 'the man.'" She sighed theatrically, and tossed the black shawl sweater was knitting into her bag. Her entire color palette was black.

Sylvia laughed, and it was a bitter sound. "Darling girl, if it were possible for us to be filmed, I'd have played the dowager Lady Grantham. I'm perfect for the part. Maggie, Judy, Helen, I'd give those dames a run for their money. But we don't appear on film any more than we show up in mirrors or photographs. You can no more be a television or film star than you can sunbathe on the Riviera."

I felt so guilty. I'd never thought that my exciting news would be such a downer for the vampires who lived beneath my Oxford shop. "I'm so sorry," I said. "I didn't think. I can cancel it."

"Don't even think of such a thing," Gran cried. "This is wonderful publicity for Cardinal Woolsey's, and for you."

"Maybe you can even learn to knit in the next two weeks," Hester said. When she was disappointed, she got mean.

I was trying to become a passable knitter even as I was trying to become a better witch. But neither of those occupations were exactly easy. At least, not for me.

However, I hadn't completely wasted the business diploma I'd earned back home in Boston. I might be a fledgling witch and an inexperienced knitter, but I wasn't half bad at running a knitting shop.

The proof was that Larch Wools had chosen Cardinal Woolsey's to be featured on television.

I wondered who the six chosen knitters would be, and whether Teddy Lamont would be as much fun as he appeared to be in his monthly magazine. I hoped so. Even his knitting patterns had personality. I was going to spend every spare minute of the next two weeks practicing my craft.

Order your copy today! *Lace and Lies* is Book 7 in the Vampire Knitting Club series.

ALSO BY NANCY WARREN

The best way to keep up with new releases, plus enjoy bonus content and prizes is to join Nancy's newsletter at NancyWarrenAuthor.com or join her in her private Facebook group Nancy Warren's Knitwits.

Vampire Knitting Club: Paranormal Cozy Mystery

Tangles and Treasons - a free prequel for Nancy's newsletter subscribers

The Vampire Knitting Club - Book 1

Stitches and Witches - Book 2

Crochet and Cauldrons - Book 3

Stockings and Spells - Book 4

Purls and Potions - Book 5

Fair Isle and Fortunes - Book 6

Lace and Lies - Book 7

Bobbles and Broomsticks - Book 8

Popcorn and Poltergeists - Book 9

Garters and Gargoyles - Book 10

Diamonds and Daggers - Book 11

Herringbones and Hexes - Book 12

Ribbing and Runes - Book 13

Cat's Paws and Curses - A Holiday Whodunnit

Vampire Knitting Club Boxed Set: Books 1-3

Vampire Knitting Club Boxed Set: Books 4-6

The Great Witches Baking Show: Culinary Cozy Mystery

The Great Witches Baking Show - Book 1

Baker's Coven - Book 2

A Rolling Scone - Book 3

A Bundt Instrument - Book 4

Blood, Sweat and Tiers - Book 5

Crumbs and Misdemeanors - Book 6

A Cream of Passion - Book 7

Cakes and Pains - Book 8

Gingerdead House - A Holiday Whodunnit

The Great Witches Baking Show Boxed Set: Books 1-3

Vampire Book Club: Paranormal Women's Fiction Cozy Mystery

Crossing the Lines - Prequel

The Vampire Book Club - Book 1

Chapter and Curse - Book 2

A Spelling Mistake - Book 3

Toni Diamond Mysteries

Toni is a successful saleswoman for Lady Bianca Cosmetics in this series of humorous cozy mysteries.

Frosted Shadow - Book 1

Ultimate Concealer - Book 2

Midnight Shimmer - Book 3

A Diamond Choker For Christmas - A Holiday Whodunnit

The Almost Wives Club

An enchanted wedding dress is a matchmaker in this series of romantic comedies where five runaway brides find out who the best men really are!

The Almost Wives Club: Kate - Book 1

Second Hand Bride - Book 2

Bridesmaid for Hire - Book 3

The Wedding Flight - Book 4

If the Dress Fits - Book 5

Take a Chance series

Meet the Chance family, a cobbled together family of eleven kids who are all grown up and finding their ways in life and love.

Chance Encounter - Prequel

Kiss a Girl in the Rain - Book 1

Iris in Bloom - Book 2

Blueprint for a Kiss - Book 3

Every Rose - Book 4

Love to Go - Book 5

The Sheriff's Sweet Surrender - Book 6

The Daisy Game - Book 7

Take a Chance Box Set - Prequel and Books 1-3

Abigail Dixon Mysteries: 1920s Cozy Historical Mystery

In 1920s Paris everything is très chic, except murder.

Death of a Flapper - Book 1

For a complete list of books, check out Nancy's website at NancyWarrenAuthor.com

ABOUT THE AUTHOR

Nancy Warren is the USA Today Bestselling author of more than 70 novels. She's originally from Vancouver, Canada, though she tends to wander and has lived in England, Italy and California at various times. While living in Oxford she dreamed up The Vampire Knitting Club. Favorite moments include being the answer to a crossword puzzle clue in Canada's National Post newspaper, being featured on the front page of the New York Times when her book Speed Dating launched Harlequin's NASCAR series, and being nominated three times for Romance Writers of America's RITA award. She has an MA in Creative Writing from Bath Spa University. She's an avid hiker, loves chocolate and most of all, loves to hear from readers!

The best way to stay in touch is to sign up for Nancy's newsletter at NancyWarrenAuthor.com or join her private Facebook group facebook.com/groups/NancyWarrenKnitwits

To learn more about Nancy and her books
NancyWarrenAuthor.com

CPSIA information can be obtained
at www.ICGtesting.com
Printed in the USA
LVHW010210211221
706819LV00009B/578

9 781928 145578